MW01613260

THE MILLION DOLLAR THERAPIST

K. LYNCH

Outskirts Press, Inc.
Denver, Colorado

The Million Dollar Therapist
All Rights Reserved.
Copyright © 2008 K. Lynch
v3.0

Outskirts Press, Inc.
http://www.outskirtspress.com

ISBN: 978-1-4327-2650-8

Outskirts Press and the "OP" logo are trademarks belonging to Outskirts Press, Inc.

PRINTED IN THE UNITED STATES OF AMERICA

TABLE OF CONTENTS

INTRODUCTION

She was leaving the gym—baggy clothes, no makeup, her hair pulled into a tight bun. She actually looked quite plain. Blending in with fellow New Yorkers on a busy day in Manhattan, you really could not tell how beautiful she really was.

Carol Lindsey had just turned 25. She was a licensed marital counselor and a single mother. With the memory of her first marriage fresh in her mind, she had no desire to ever consider a second, let alone to actually have contact with the male sex.

Her ex-husband, **John**, was a good-looking divorce attorney with the firm Berkowitz, Blakemore and Cohen, lately referred to as BBC. He was one of the youngest partners in the firm. He was also the most stingy and narcissistic, but only she knew that, for now.

They had been divorced less than six months. She was struggling with family duties as well as her new practice as a marital counselor. Her son, Jason, had just turned three. She drove a used Honda Civic. It wasn't easy. Her ex was making a high six-figure income. She, in turn, was getting

$250 per month for support and trying to generate an income as a marital counselor. "One of the perks of being a divorce attorney," she would muse to herself. "You get to make the rules."

Despite this, she was making ends meet. She had arranged a small loan from her bank to set up her practice. The interest was pretty stiff, but she felt she would pay it off quickly once she started generating income. From this loan she had paid four months' tuition for Jason at one of the premier preschools in the Manhattan area. "Things will be getting better soon," she would say to herself. "They just can't get worse."

She had no idea what was in store for her.

CHAPTER 1
THE BEGINNINGS

Carol Lindsey was born to a farming family in Cedar Plains, Iowa. Her parents had been farmers on the same land they inherited from her father's parents, who had inherited the land from their parents.

Life was hard and unforgiving. There was no such thing as a 40-hour work week. You didn't get coffee breaks, and time for lunch was a rarity. There was no assigned vacation, let alone a free weekend. "Sick days" were not an option. You would get up at 4 a.m. and begin work. At 7 a.m. breakfast would be ready. You would have about 15 minutes. The rest of the day would be filled with various tasks. If you were lucky you would grab a sandwich or two, and you would make certain you got plenty of water. Whether it was winter or summer, you would sweat endlessly. Dinner would be served about 7 p.m. You would eat and then drag yourself off to bed. Daily bathing was a commodity reserved for the women. This went on seven days a week. On Sunday there would be a three-hour space for going to church. Occasionally, you would take off a Sunday afternoon if there was a church picnic, ice cream social, wedding, or a funeral. Otherwise, Sunday was just another day.

This was life in the farming community, unchanged for generations. You either pulled your own weight, or you went elsewhere.

Carol's mother, Margaret, had been told she could not have children. This made it harder to maintain a farm. But there were fewer mouths to feed, and her dad, Harold, made up the difference by working harder.

Shortly after her 41st birthday, Margaret could feel herself tiring more easily. Her last period had been somewhat irregular—this was not anything particularly new, nor was the fact she was late. She thought this was "the change of life" coming on. She had seen it in her mother, except her mother had been a little older when it happened. When she detected a little more fullness in her lower abdomen, she began to worry. Her mother had died of ovarian cancer, and she knew it was hereditary. Harold and Margaret were very devoted to each other—no one kept secrets. When she told Harold of her "problem," he insisted she see their doctor immediately.

CHAPTER 2
GOOD NEWS?

"**M**rs. Lindsey." The doctor beamed. "You're pregnant!"

Margaret almost fainted. "But, Dr. Chalmers," she stammered, "you and the other specialist told me I could not have children."

"Medicine is not an exact science," he chided. "We are not always one hundred percent correct. But there is no question you are going to have a baby."

Harold beamed with the news. He refused to let Margaret do her normal chores and hired one of the ladies in town with what little savings they had—a nice widow by the name of Mrs. Praxton.

Despite this, however, Margaret tried her best to keep up her routine. "Harold," Margaret would say, "as soon as our baby is born you will have to let Mrs. Praxton go so we can start saving again."

This went on right up to the day she went into labor.

CHAPTER 3
THE DELIVERY

Labor pains came on rather suddenly for Margaret. She awoke to feel a dull ache in her lower back, followed shortly by what felt like a shock radiating down both of her legs. Right after that her water broke.

By the time Harold came home and got her to Parkland Hospital, she was in full labor. It was the most excruciating pain she had ever known.

After 12 hours of pure agonizing discomfort, the doctor took Harold aside.

"I'm afraid we are going to have to operate," he began cautiously. "The baby hasn't moved, and we can see on our new heart rate monitor that the baby's heart rate is dropping. This is a sign of fetal distress. I'm going to have to call a specialist for assistance. We must arrange for transfer to the university hospital. Thirty-five years of practice and I feel out of my league."

"By all means," Harold said, "do whatever is necessary."

He could feel his throat tightening. He hated being this helpless.

At exactly 12 midnight, Carol was delivered at the university hospital by Caesarean section. There were no problems. Her father felt a great weight had been lifted from his shoulders. "Thank you, God," he said silently.

Two days later, Margaret was up and demanding to leave. "I've ignored our home long enough," she protested. "I don't care what the doctors say. These younger doctors don't know anything anyway…and I don't care if this is the university hospital. I will only listen to my own doctor."

"Mrs. Lindsey," the resident said, trying to comfort her. "You should remain at least two more days. Your baby needs at least one more day in the nursery, and I don't want your stitches to come out prematurely. I know what you're going to do as soon as you get home."

"I don't care," Margaret protested. "I want my doctor."

They finally relented and called Dr. Chalmers. It was 10:30 p.m. by the time they located him. He was about 40 miles from Des Moines.

"Dr. Chalmers," the resident began, "she just won't listen to reason. Could you please come over and talk to her?"

"You mean you don't have any medicine that will make her listen to reason?" Dr. Chalmers said sarcastically. "Maybe you should order an MRI or something—that will take up the rest of the night. How about one of those newfangled computerized angiograms of her head to make sure she is getting enough circulation to the brain? Hell, I've been up for the last twenty-three hours. Don't you ivory tower types have any kind of bedside manner?"

(Dr. Chalmers was really relishing his situation here. For years he had tried to get a formal appointment other than "courtesy staff" from these university snobs. Now he was actually being asked to participate in the care of a patient he had referred to them. Admittedly, the request was only coming from the chief resident, but he enjoyed the acknowledgement anyway. Up until now he had been treated like a second class citizen. He was extracting payback.)

"Please," the chief resident begged. "I will wait for you at the reception desk myself. I will even call the chief of staff to see that you are granted emergency privileges."

"Okay. But I want to spend the rest of the night in the senior staff quarters. And make sure they have fresh towels and soap," he snapped. "And I want the valet parking kept open. I'm not going to park a mile away like the last time."

"Absolutely," the resident responded. His throat tightened. "Whatever you want. Just come talk to her."

Dr. Chalmers arrived within the hour. He had donned a starched white lab coat with his name sewn on the chest pocket. He looked every bit like a "senior staff man."

The chief resident met him in the lounge.

"Where's my coffee?" Dr. Chalmers snapped. "I've been going at it for the last twenty-four hours. I'm not like you young guys."

Obediently, the resident disappeared and returned with fresh coffee.

Dr. Chalmers took a sip and made a face. "This tastes like the crankcase oil in my tractor!"

"Please, Dr. Chalmers," the resident said meekly, "let me escort you up to OB."

CHAPTER 4
THE UNIVERSITY HOSPITAL

The OB-GYN floor was carpeted. Not like the stark tile floors at Parkland. Instead of plain green walls, there were paintings—mostly Impressionist reproductions, but beautifully done.

Margaret had a private room. A television was mounted on the wall with a remote control built into her bed. She was still trying to figure out how to work it when Dr. Chalmers was escorted in by the resident.

"Margaret," he began gently. "You really need to take it easy for at least another two days. You have not had a free day in the last thirty years—just another two days is all I would ask."

Margaret listened to him and finally agreed. Dr. Chalmers had been their family doctor since she could remember. He also came from a farming community roughly 40 miles north of Cedar Plains. He had a huge practice that covered four counties. He knew the work ethic ingrained in the people in his practice from his own parents.

CHAPTER 5
HOME AGAIN

O n a windy Friday morning, Carol arrived in her first home.

There wasn't much time for fanfare. Some neighbors would come by in the evening with gifts or casseroles. Harold and Margaret decided to keep Mrs. Praxton on. She and Margaret had begun making pear and apricot preserves and selling the extra jars in town. Soon, things were back to their routine. At least as routine as it can be with a new baby.

Then the bills from the doctors and the hospital began to come. Back then you paid for your medical care. There were no health plans or government "programs."

The bills from Dr. Chalmers were the usual routine. He charged $50 for monitoring Margaret during the first stages of her delivery and an additional $25 for the trip to the university hospital.

The local hospital was a little more stiff—$844 for the one-day stay prior to transfer, plus some other "creative" charges—$45 for pharmacy review (Margaret had been given a stool softener), $25 for nurse chart review, $33 for record copying, etc. The total was just under $1,000.

The university hospital charges were astronomical. The bill was 22 pages long, with miscellaneous charges ranging from $53 for a dental hygiene kit, consisting of a toothbrush and a small tube of toothpaste, to $5,378 for the operating room. The total stood out in bold black letters at the bottom of page 22: **$25,488.**

"For that," Harold said, "we could have cruised around the world in the Queen Mary."

Harold simply arranged a loan with his local bank, putting up most of his land as collateral. With his hard work, and the small extra income they were getting from the sale of the preserves, they eventually paid the loan in full. He never questioned the charges, although $53 for a toothbrush and toothpaste seemed a little strange. The university hospital averaged over 15,000 admissions a year. Regardless of the nature of the admission, each patient received a dental hygiene kit for a profit of about $50 dollars per kit. The total net income to the hospital was about $750,000 per year. This was only the tip of the iceberg. Such charges are common to every hospital in the country.

CHAPTER 6
THE EARLY DAYS

For the first few months, Harold could barely keep his mind on the farm. Certainly there were the usual chores—nothing changed there. But he worked with a renewed vitality. He managed to come by the house five or six times during the day—always with some excuse. Obviously, it was only to see his new little girl.

"Harold," Margaret would chide, "she needs her nap…"

"I won't disturb her," he replied. "I just want to see her, and I think I left my new shears in the kitchen."

"You know perfectly well they are hanging in the woodshed," Margaret said, laughing aloud. She knew he was running out of excuses.

CHAPTER 7
CAROL

Carol was a beautiful child. She had the best features of both her parents. She was her father's pride and joy. In a very short time, however, they could see she was a little bit more than "normal."

"Margaret," Mrs. Praxton said excitedly one day, "this child knows the recipes for our preserves by heart!"

And it was true. At the age of three, Carol had learned to read right from their recipe book. By age five she had learned to add by sitting on her father's lap when he was doing the books.

The first five years for Carol were idyllic. She would get up in the morning, have breakfast, and then join her father in the barn as he hooked the cows up to a newfangled milking machine they had just bought. She adored her father, but really did not see him enough.

"Harold," Margaret would say at night, "Carol is going to

have to begin school. You have had her to yourself for the last five years. She needs to be with children her own age."

"I know, Margaret. We have the best public schools in the state, but I can't get used to the idea of her ever leaving home. And anyway, she just turned five."

Carol was the absolute center of their lives. Mrs. Praxton had taken on the role of an aunt. From the time Carol learned to talk, she called her "Aunt P." And Aunt P adored Carol as one of her own.

From the time Carol was enrolled in the first grade, her abilities really began to shine through.

The town schoolmaster, Mr. Rolands, had been born and raised in Cedar Plains. He was known for being very strict and somewhat aloof. He had a flare for drama from his various roles in the Shakespearean personae. He often lamented he should have opted for a stage career.

Part of this was true. He had turned down a teaching grant at Wellsley in favor of becoming the schoolmaster for Cedar Rapids. However, his abilities on stage were in doubt.

"Mrs. Lindsey," the schoolmaster began one afternoon, "Carol is after my job. She is teaching the sixth graders how to read and do math. What is more disconcerting is that she does it better than me. She knows how to talk to them since she is their age. She even tutors the seventh and eighth graders." He buried his head in his hands in feigned frustration.

Margaret was not particularly moved by his dramatization. She was a practical woman and knew the schoolmaster from when they went to school together. She simply folded her arms and looked at him.

"I would like to have her tested for our accelerated programs," he continued, shedding his shroud of exaggeration.

"That is wonderful news, Mr. Rolands," exclaimed Mrs. Lindsey. "However, I will have to talk it over with Harold."

"Absolutely not!" Harold had exclaimed that evening on learning of the news. "Our daughter is not a test tube for a bunch of professor wannabes to use for their experiments."

"But, Harold," Margaret said, "she is several years ahead of her class. This could only help her."

"Oh, all right," he relented. "But I am not letting her leave home for one of those new fancy schools in Des Moines. She just isn't ready."

"You mean, Harold, *you're* not ready." Margaret measured her words carefully. Carol had been the center of his life. Even as a devoted husband, Margaret knew that when Carol left, she might see a change in Harold.

Carol did very well on the accelerated program's pretest. In fact she excelled over the 300 or so students who had been selected as the best in their classes. The experts recommended she be enrolled in their finest teaching center in Des Moines.

"I won't hear of it," Harold said. "Our daughter is a gift from God. I am not ready to share her with anyone else."

That was pretty much the final word. Margaret knew better than to push him any further right now. Carol was destined to stay home and advance normally through the local school system. After that, she would belong to the world. Even Harold knew that.

Evenings were always special to Carol. She would come home from school, help her mother and Mrs. Praxton with dinner, and then wait for her father.

He would always get home by 7 p.m., rain or shine. His only thoughts would be of his family, and evenings were precious. They were never going to be rich, but after paying off the hospital bills, he had begun to save a small amount every month. When the time came, he would be able to afford one of those expensive eastern schools for Carol. He did not look forward to the day she would leave, but he knew it was inevitable. Little did he know how close he would come to losing her.

CHAPTER 8
TRAGEDY

Summers were particularly exciting for Carol—no school, no homework, and no teachers making her take a new line of aptitude tests. Summertime was for being with her mom and dad. Many farm chores had to be done—even with the extra hired help, it seemed the list was endless.

Carol's main chore in the morning was to hook up the cows to the milk extractors. She was very gentle and very adept at placing the suction cups. Each cow had a name—Hannibal, Jennifer, Cindy…and so on.

Harold and Margaret had purchased a prize bull when they first began to manage the farm. They nicknamed him Raoule. Raoule had fathered many calves in his time. But he was getting older, and Harold figured he was now just "shooting blanks." Despite this, Hannibal had somehow gotten pregnant. Obviously Raoule had one last shot left. Hannibal had become very irritable and required special care.

One early morning Carol absentmindedly stood directly behind Hannibal while freeing up the tubes to the milking machine. Without hesitation, Hannibal kicked backward, striking Carol just to the left of her forehead. Carol flew across the barn and landed ten feet away. She was unconscious before she hit the ground.

When Carol did not respond to the breakfast bell, Margaret came out looking for her. She was the first to find her lying in the straw, barely breathing. Margaret's screams rousted Harold and the other hands, who came running to the barn.

Margaret was cradling Carol's fragile body in her arms, crying hysterically. Harold fell to his knees. *She's dead*, he thought. Upon seeing Harold's distressed look, Margaret snapped to her senses and took control.

"Get the car," she snapped. "I will not let her die like this."

In less than an instant Harold had pulled his pickup truck in front of the barn and they sped off to the hospital. A light rain had just begun to fall.

Parkland General had always been a good hospital, serving the needs of the local community, which to now had numbered about 10,000. They had a fully staffed emergency room, a state-of-the-art CAT scanner, and specialists on call.

Except for a neurosurgeon.

CHAPTER 9
DR. BRIELY

Dr. Briely had been the neurosurgeon for Parkland and several of the other local hospitals in the past. He had trained at Massachusetts General and began his career in his home state of Iowa. He was dedicated, precise, and domineering, as is any good surgeon operating on people's brains and spines. He was handsome, well liked, and very successful. He had married his high school sweetheart, a prom queen, and they settled in a beautiful mansion they were restoring. They were starting to talk of raising a family.

However, after the first five years of practice, the stress of being solo and the tragedies he sometimes faced began to take their toll.

It was common knowledge that Dr. Briely had a weakness for fine wines and champagne. In fact, he had one of the most prestigious wine cellars in Iowa. In the evening he would have one or two glasses with his wife before going to bed.

After a rare vacation to the Bordeaux region of France with his wife, he had purchased a case of a perfectly aged Cabernet Sauvignon, a Chateau Geron. When it arrived, he and his wife opened the first bottle enthusiastically.

"My God!" he had exclaimed. "This is one of the most perfect cabs I have ever tasted. This is about the only thing the French do right!" His wife did not agree, feeling there was too much of an oak aftertaste, considering what they had paid. She went up to take a bath, leaving him to finish the bottle.

Dr. Briely currently did not have any patients in the hospitals he covered. He was on call, but rarely did he receive any after-midnight calls.

Tonight, however, was going to be different.

The phone rang at 12:10 a.m. "Dr. Briely," the excited ER doctor began, "we have a sixteen-year-old male who sustained blunt head trauma in an auto accident. His tox screen is positive for methamphetamines and marijuana. The CT shows an acute subdural hematoma. His left pupil is dilated, and he has already had one seizure."

Dr. Briely lived about 40 minutes from the hospital. After clearing his head, he muttered, "Call in the OR team now and have that CT scan in the OR for me—I'll need to look at the films."

"The radiologist has already read out the study," the ER doctor added. "I have his wet reading."

"I don't give a holy damn!" Dr. Briely barked back. "Unless the radiologist wants to do the craniotomy, you have those films in the OR by the time I get there."

"Yes sir!" the ER doc responded. However, something was not right. He had heard Dr. Briely yell and carry on in the ER, but he had never heard him swear.

Dr. Briely arrived, spoke with the distressed parents briefly, and hurried to the OR, assuring them that everything would be fine. He would perform a craniotomy and evacuate the hematoma, taking the pressure off their son's brain. This was a common procedure, even in community hospitals. He had done this hundreds of times under urgent circumstances and had never lost a patient. It was only later that the mother recalled he was chewing a breath mint. The underlying scent of alcohol was unmistakable. Several of the hospital personnel had gotten the same impression.

The surgery was initiated without a hitch. The anesthesiologist put the young man under, the scrub nurse shaved his head, the circulating nurse made certain the young man was hooked up to all the fancy monitors…and the orderly put up the films on the view box. The radiologist's wet reading was taped to the bottom of one of the films. The scrawled report was almost illegible: L SDH (left subdural hematoma).

In the hospital hierarchy, the orderly is usually the youngest and least experienced person on the OR team. He generally is a high school graduate, and, in this case, was a college student in his second year of pre-med at Penn State.

Admittedly, the labeling on the film was obscure. Each picture of the brain was surrounded with fine print describing the thickness of the section imaged, the technique, the acquisition, and even the manufacturer of the CT machine. In all this pointless fine print, the right or left marker showing which side of brain was damaged was lost. Not knowing this, and feeling the urgency of the situation, the orderly felt good about just getting the films up.

Dr. Briely assessed the young man before him. He had an obvious abrasion over his right scalp, along with other cuts and scrapes on his face. He had already been put under by the anesthesiologist, and a Vaseline-coated tape had been placed over his eyelids. Dr. Briely did not bother to check the pupils.

He briefly eyed the films across the room and agreed the young man had a rather large subdural hematoma. He glanced at the note the radiologist had scrawled, but could not read the writing. Besides, he had reviewed many CAT scans of the brain and felt he was better at reading them than any radiologist.

Because of the size of the subdural hematoma, Dr. Briely made a large curvilinear incision over the right side of the young man's head where the abrasion was. Even after almost a full bottle of wine, his hands were controlled, their movements precise. He then strategically used the equivalent of a small power saw to cut through the skull bone. After removing this large section of bone, he set it aside, noting that the remaining white dura showed no real signs of discoloration or bulging. *This must be smaller than it seems on the CAT scan*, he thought. *Probably the angle of the image...*

The dura is a thick, protective covering immediately overlying the brain containing the reservoir of fluid which acts as a cushion around the brain.

Again, with experienced, precise hands, he incised the dura, exposing the brain itself. To his horror, there was no blood over the brain as the CAT scan had shown—just the clear fluid. He dropped his scalpel and ran over to the view box, scrutinizing the films. It was only then he saw the films were put up backward.

"Who the hell put these films up?" he shouted. His sea-soned OR crew was silent. The orderly had long since left to transport other patients to and from their destinations. "I've got to do a contralateral craniotomy!" he exclaimed.

But now the situation was deteriorating. The pressure on the left side of the brain had pushed the normal right side of the brain through the large hole in the skull. The normal brain bulged out, trying to follow the path of least resis-tance. Massive seizure activity began to be recorded on all the monitors. With pressure building up in the deep parts of the brain, the heart rate began to slow inexorably.

"We're losing him!" the anesthesiologist shouted. A sick-ening silence fell across the room.

Dr. Briely did his contralateral craniotomy in record time, exposing the large jello-like mass of clotted blood that had been pushing on the left half of the brain. He quickly evacuated the blood in an attempt to relieve the pressure.

But it was too late. When someone gets even a minor blow to the head, the injured soft tissue will swell. The brain is no different. When injured, it will swell. The fancy name for this is cerebral edema. In this case both sides of the young man's brain began to swell uncontrollably. Urgent measures to control cerebral edema would consist of steroids (corti-sone) and water pills to cause dehydration. The neuroprotec-tive medicines—medications that could strengthen the walls of the brain cells—had yet to be discovered. The steroids and the water pills would take time to act. But here, time had run out. The central part of the brain controlling heart rate, temperature, and blood pressure was now damaged beyond repair. The heart slowed down, the blood pressure dropped, and the body began to overheat. Despite the efforts of the experienced anesthesiologist, all resuscitation efforts failed.

For the next few minutes, no one really said anything. There was nothing to say. The brilliant, precise, half-intoxicated neurosurgeon had botched the operation. He now had to face the family. Forget the fact the young man had been taking meth and driving recklessly. As the physician in charge, he was responsible for this patient's death.

With his shoulders hunched, and looking at the floor, Dr. Briely walked down the long, stark hallway to where the parents were clutching each other apprehensively. Before he could even mumble his first words, the mother began to sob uncontrollably. From that point on, nothing he said could be heard.

Over the next few weeks the case was reviewed by the various hospital committees—the Quality Care Committee, the Risk Review Committee, the Surgery Review Committee, and so on. Each committee went over the facts of the case and promptly passed it on to the next committee. Two absolute facts stood out as if carved in stone—the neurosurgeon had an unmistakable scent of alcohol on his breath, and he had operated on the wrong side of the brain. The scent of alcohol could be dismissed as hearsay, even though everyone knew Dr. Briely did like his wines. However, drunk or sober, he had performed a craniotomy on the wrong side, which had led to the patient's death.

The entire case was finally passed up to the Medical Executive Committee for a decision.

"We can't suspend him!" the chief of staff exclaimed. "He is the only neurosurgeon around this area, plus he serves three other hospitals." This was a real dilemma faced at smaller hospitals in rural areas. "He operated based on what he saw on the films! Up until now his track record has been flawless."

A silence gripped the room, only to be broken by the hospital attorney. "If we don't act decisively, we are looking at a major lawsuit."

While all this was going on, the family had retained a local attorney, who, realizing the value of this case, sought out a large firm in Des Moines that had made a fortune suing doctors.

"I am obligated to consult with the best counsel I can find," the local attorney told the grieving parents. "Your son should be at home with you." Deep inside, he was gloating over his new fortune.

The truth was he could have cared less about his clients. He was a typical attorney who could see only money and positive notoriety. He knew some attorneys who had made millions of dollars capitalizing on the misfortunes of others. He was no different than any other graduate coming out of law school. This was his chance to make it big. He relished his moment in the sun—being able to capitalize on the parents' grief.

In addition to the multimillion-dollar malpractice suit directed at both Dr. Briely and the hospital, the firm filed a wrongful death suit against Dr. Briely. Within a few weeks, the local newspaper ran the story. "Intoxicated Neurosurgeon Operates on the Wrong Side of the Brain..."

The story spread like wildfire. Soon it was on the front page of major newspapers around the country. **YOUNG MAN DIES AT HANDS OF INTOXICATED NEUROSURGEON.**

Dr. Briely's malpractice company was less than supportive. "You will have to settle," his attorney told him. "The case is indefensible. I can dismiss the alleged alcohol abuse on your part since no tests were run and it would be simply hearsay. However, I can't defend the fact that you cut into the wrong side of the head. Furthermore, I have no say in the final decision by the state board of medical examiners. Your coverage, Doctor, is only for one point five million. With punitive damages, they could get over ten times that amount!"

Shortly after the first few interviews with the hospital committees and his malpractice company, Dr. Briely took a leave of absence and fell into a deep depression. His colleagues did their best to support him, but he was belligerent to anyone who came near him. His wife left to stay with her mother. At least until this blew over and he came to his senses.

But that did not happen. Dr. Briely began to take large doses of sedatives in order to sleep. He refused to see anyone. His only escape became his wine cellar.

After three days of no calls or messages, his wife returned to their home. She found him sprawled in the corner of his wine cellar, unconscious and unarousable. His once handsome face was contorted in pain. A large bruise was on his forehead. Several bottles of the Chateau Geron lay empty next to him.

The coroner estimated he had been dead for at least 36 hours. Ironically, at autopsy they found a large right-sided subdural hematoma.

CHAPTER 10
THE FLIGHT

Harold and Margaret knew nothing of the events at Parkland Hospital and the fate of Dr. Briely. That had been several years ago.

The rain was coming down very hard as they pulled into the parking lot. Gasping, Harold carried the limp body of his daughter into the emergency room.

The ER physician on duty was Dr. Thompson. He was four years out of training as an ER specialist. He placed Carol on a gurney and began an immediate assessment. She had obvious swelling over her left eye. Her left pupil was dilated and did not constrict to the small light he flashed into it.

He first placed a small breathing tube down her throat since her respirations were now becoming too shallow. The nurse started an IV, and they took her over to the Radiology Department for a CAT scan. Just before leaving she received an IV push of Decadron—a type of cortisone designed to minimize swelling in acute brain injuries. He also ordered a vial of acetyl carnitine. This was a new agent that had just been approved by the FDA to sort of "shore up" the microscopic walls of damaged brain cells.

The CAT scan showed an obvious left-sided subdural hematoma pushing the brain to the right.

*She needs to have this evacuated imm*ediately, the ER doctor thought. *But the nearest neurosurgeon is over 60 miles away. That would be at least an hour by ambulance. It would be too late then...*

Doctors frequently have to transfer critical patients to the university hospital. However, in this case, every minute counted.

In the midst of his dilemma, he remembered that his uncle was a helicopter pilot who was doing his obligatory six weeks with the local National Guard. Major Bernam was a decorated Vietnam veteran and a survivor of many close calls. He had over five thousand hours in both Cobras and Apache helicopters. The Guard had just received a new fleet of Blackhawks. The base was less than a mile from the hospital.

"Hey, Doc," the major exclaimed to his nephew. "Have you looked outside lately? We're having one of those summer storms right now. Winds are estimated to be over forty knots. Can't you arrange ground transportation?"

"Major!" Dr. Thompson said, gritting his teeth. "If this little girl is not in an OR with a neurosurgical team in thirty minutes, the mode of transportation will be academic."

Major Bernam could feel the stress in his voice. "Okay, Doc—relax! The cavalry is on its way," he said, feeling the urgency of the situation. "And, by the way…cut back on that coffee."

In less than five minutes Major Bernam had landed his Blackhawk in the parking lot with his med evac team. Carol was rushed to the helicopter through the rain. The turbulence from the helicopter blades made the winds seem even stronger. A lawn chair was blown into one of the glass doors of the ER, narrowly missing Margaret. Both Harold and Margaret insisted on boarding the helicopter. Harold even pushed aside one of the paramedics who was standing in their way.

The trip to the university hospital was the closest thing to a roller-coaster ride that Harold and Margaret had ever experienced. The wind howled relentlessly. The rain limited the visibility to less than 500 feet.

Major Bernam's copilot was a 2nd lieutenant just out of the academy. "Sir! Shouldn't we turn back? We are well below IFR."

IFR was short for instrument flight rules. The military was strict about this and for good reason. Major Bernam's decision to fly through the storm was an emotional one. If he had ever done this in Vietnam, he would have been blown out of the sky. But this was very different.

"Son," Major Bernam said without hesitation, "this is no different than flying in a monsoon in SEA (Southeast Asia). Look at the bright side—no one's shooting at us!"

The harrowing flight took less than 15 minutes. Harold fought back the overwhelming desire to get sick all over the inside of the helicopter. He just focused on Carol. *Please, God,* he thought, *I have never asked for anything…just don't let my little girl die.*

Major Bernam set the chopper on the helipad next to the university emergency room without blinking an eye. The wind howled as the paramedics rushed Carol to the emergency room, followed closely by Harold and Margaret.

"You can let go of the stick now, Lieutenant," Major Bernam said to his co-pilot. But the young lieutenant sat frozen in his seat watching the rain beating down on the glass canopy. He did not respond to the order.

The army sent a truck to pick up the reserve unit. Major Bernam received a severe reprimand from the base commander for flying through such bad weather. "This isn't the first time you've bent the rules, Major," the grizzled commander began, "but it will be your last while you are under my command!"

However, upon later learning that the bridge over the Mokulume River had been washed out by the freak storm that morning, the letter of reprimand evaporated. Besides, the publicity was overwhelming, and the entire crew, including the lieutenant, was given the Unit Citation Medal.

CHAPTER 11
THE OPERATION

T he neurosurgical team was ready. The neurosurgeon, the anesthesiologist, the chief resident, the scrub nurse, and the circulating nurse all moved like a well-oiled machine. With the notoriety of Dr. Briely's error, hospitals had changed their policy. Everything was reviewed, scrutinized, and re-reviewed. It was now the duty of the operating surgeon to write the word "yes" with a sterile marking pen on the side of the patient undergoing the surgery. Regardless of the urgency of the situation, the scrub nurse would not hand the scalpel to the surgeon unless this was done. The films and report were also reviewed. No longer would the letter R or L suffice in the wet reading. The word right or left had to be clearly printed. Before the first incision was made, the surgeon would have to clearly announce the name of the patient and the procedure he was to perform, including the specific area. This was dubbed a "Time Out." It was to become a universal practice.

The operation was begun immediately after Carol's arrival. The surgeon made his incision through the soft tissues of the scalp, and the resident suctioned and cauterized the incision. The anesthesiologist had his eyes locked on the digital printouts of his monitors.

The bone flap was elevated in a matter of minutes. The surgeon could see the purple bulge underneath the dura. He incised the dura and aspirated the jello-like collection of clotted blood, being careful not to touch the exposed brain. He then watched for any signs of potential bleeding.

"Okay, people! Time to close up!" The neurosurgeon's voice seemed to break the chill that had gripped the OR.

The bone flap was fixed to the rest of the skull with filamentous wire sutures. Each layer of tissue covering the scalp was then selectively closed. A small rubber drain was left in the space where the clot had accumulated, just in case there was more bleeding. This could be removed easily in the next two days. Additional doses of Decadron and acetyl carnitine were administered.

Carol was then transported to the intensive care unit. She remained hooked up to several monitors constantly checking her blood pressure, heart rate, and blood oxygen. A machine inflated and deflated her small lungs with a careful mixture of oxygen, nitrogen, and carbon dioxide. Not enough oxygen could further damage her already injured brain cells. Too much carbon dioxide would cause the microscopic blood vessels in her brain to dilate and possibly rupture. Everything had to be precise. The machines dwarfed her small body.

Harold and Margaret kept a vigil at Carol's bedside. Mrs. Praxton brought their meals and sat with them. Over the next 48 hours, Carol was on full life support. The machines hummed in the background. No one spoke.

By the fourth day, however, Carol began to move.

"She is moving all four extremities normally," the neurosurgeon said cautiously. "And she is breathing on her own. I think we can remove the breathing tube…"

Once the breathing tube was removed, Carol appeared more natural. One less machine in the room. She still did not open her eyes.

However, on the sixth day her eyes fluttered open. "Daddy," she said with her first words. "Please don't blame Hannibal. It was my fault for standing too close…"

Tears of joy streamed down his weathered face. This was the first time she had ever seen tears from her father.

"Honey," he began, "it isn't anyone's fault. We're just thankful to have you back."

Four more days in the hospital and Carol was ready to go home. One by one all the machines were taken from the room.

The trip home was a joyful one—much different from the drive to the emergency room at Parkland.

Once home, everything took on a routine sequence. Hannibal gave birth to twin calves and began to produce twice as much milk as the others.

Carol gradually began to take on more responsibility with the running of the farm. She noticed, however, that when she felt a little stressed, her forehead would begin to hurt.

CHAPTER 12
TIME PASSES

Up through her junior year Carol did not date anyone. She was too busy with school, gymnastics, and, of course, her family. However, early in her junior year she met Roger.

They were both independently working out for the next gymnastics meet with their longstanding rival. She noticed him watching her on the power rings. She was proud of her skill on them, but he made her feel self-conscious and she lost her concentration. She thought she saw him laugh.

After showering, she ran into him again outside the gym.

"You looked really good in there," he remarked.

"I recall seeing you laugh," she shot back.

"Oh, no." He appeared shocked. "I was just surprised by your ability. I haven't seen anyone do those rings as well as you—not even the upperclassmen. Please," Roger said, "we are both dehydrated. Maybe we could stop by The Buzz for a lemon Coke."

The Buzz was the local hangout for most of the kids in town. Carol rarely went there. They did have good sundaes and the best French fries in Iowa.

"I can't." Carol hesitated. "I have really got to get home."

"Carol," Roger persisted. "Please...I would really like to get to know you."

Roger was very handsome and tall for being just 17. He had sharp, chiseled features, blond hair, and a very muscular build. What Carol found nice was that he didn't flaunt it. His shirts were loose—not like the skintight tops some of the gymnasts wore. He had grown a lot over the last year and had a lanky, slightly uncoordinated appearance. But Carol could see he was a genuine person.

"All right," she relented, "but I can only spare twenty minutes."

"Twenty minutes, then." Roger beamed.

The rendezvous at The Buzz became a regular thing for Carol and Roger. They became fast friends. Carol felt very attracted to him and began to experience things she could not understand. Things she could never even mention to her mother.

Roger and Carol had been dating for almost six months. Both parents approved. Roger had been accepted to Johns Hopkins' undergrad program, where he would be starting his premed studies. He was a hard worker.

By the fourth date, he had made a distinct effort to kiss her. At 17 she had never been kissed. The feel of his warm lips and his muscular body again ignited those feelings she had rarely experienced. At first, she pulled back, but then she gave in to an overwhelming desire to be close to him. Over the next few months, they saw each other constantly. When they were alone, they would kiss passionately. One evening he tried to get his hand on her breast. This was met with a sharp slap to his cheek. He never tried to do that again. Not, at least, until the evening of the prom.

CHAPTER 13
THE PROM

The prom was classically in late spring. The weather was always accommodating that time of year. The dance was the highlight of the year. The whole town was abuzz over it. The guys would be outfitted in rented tuxedos. The girls would get the most elaborate gowns their families could afford.

On the night of the prom, Margaret and Mrs. Praxton pranced around Carol like two fairy godmothers. Mrs. Praxton had sewn a special dress for her, and Margaret had designed seven silk yellow roses that went diagonally from her shoulders to her slim waist. The final fitting took place over a two-hour period, much to Harold's amusement. He didn't really mind if dinner was late. It was the first time in over 30 years of marriage, and it was worth it.

"Margaret," he said, "if you had told me dinner would be late, I would have sent out to that new pizza place in town."

Margaret glared at him. "Harold, all you have to do is open

the oven and take it out! You remember where the oven is in the kitchen. And don't spill anything!"

"Margaret," Harold shouted from the kitchen, "what did you do with the pot holders? It's been so long since I have been in this kitchen, I just can't remember."

"I am not amused," she exclaimed. With that she turned and went back to her duties as fairy godmother. When she and Mrs. Praxton were finished, Carol looked like a fashion model in an original Dior. The dress had a radiant white sheen and was accentuated by the seven roses. In truth, the New York designers would have killed for a dress like this.

The evening was a fantasy night for Carol. Roger had rented a powder blue tuxedo. He was the most handsome man she had ever seen.

After the prom was underway and they had danced the first few dances, they got a glass of punch and sat alone in the corner of the dance floor.

"Let's get some air," Roger said.

The outside breeze was perfect. Seeing they were alone, he again kissed her. Carol kissed him back fervently, stroking the back of his head. He pulled her closer to him. The feel of his muscular body sent a wave of passion through her. They danced the last few dances barely moving from one spot.

The last dance ended at 11 p.m. It was an unwritten rule you would have your date home by midnight or there-abouts...

"Maybe we could stop by my parents' house," he volunteered. Carol knew his parents were out of town for the weekend.

"Okay," she said, "but just for a little while…"

They slipped into his home quietly and sat on the couch.

"Could I get you a Coke?" Roger volunteered.

"No, I'm fine," she said. But she could feel her heart pounding involuntarily inside her chest.

Again he began to kiss her passionately, and again, Carol felt herself spinning out of control. She wasn't certain what was going to happen. Every touch from him made her body tingle. She found herself running her hand over the bulge between his legs. She knew what she was feeling; she just didn't know it could feel so hard. She only had heard stories from her friends.

Roger unbuttoned her gown and slipped it off her. It lay next to her on the couch. She was only in her lingerie, leaving little to the imagination. He held her closely, running his hands over her smooth skin. He reached behind her and unhooked her bra. Her nipples stood out firmly, accentuated by the pale moonlight shining through the window. He encircled her right nipple with his mouth, running his tongue around it. Now, she was at the point of no return. She was completely entranced. What was happening almost seemed unreal. Somehow he had completely disrobed and was sitting next to her, naked. She instinctively moved her right hand over his lower abdomen and began stroking him as they kissed. She could feel his body begin to tremble.

Suddenly she felt a warm gush of fluid coming from him,

literally shooting through her fingers and landing on her gown. She stood up abruptly—horrified. She grabbed her gown and ran into the bathroom. She scrubbed furiously at the large puddle of fluid that had instantly settled into the satin. She must have washed the spot for ten minutes straight. She was mortified.

She emerged without saying a word. Roger had already dressed. She dressed quietly, trying to hold back her tears. They drove to her home in silence. Roger tried to say something as they pulled up to the front gate, but Carol was not listening.

Carol's parents and Mrs. Praxton were fast asleep. It had been a long day for them—also for Carol. She slipped quietly into her room and went to bed.

CHAPTER 14
THE DAY AFTER

The next day when Carol awoke, she immediately held her gown up to the light. To her horror there was a distinctive stain. She had not washed it thoroughly enough.

Carol was subdued at breakfast. "I guess I'm still a little tired," she had volunteered. Nothing further was said.

That afternoon, however, the phone rang, and Margaret answered.

"Carol, that was Mr. Rolands. He wants to come over this evening and discuss something. He sounded very serious."

Carol felt her knees growing weak. She was certain the whole town would know what had transpired. A limitless number of irrational scenarios ran through her mind. "You will now be known as the hand job queen of Cedar High," a little voice said inside her. Her forehead began to pound.

Fortunately, her apprehensions were misdirected.

Mr. Rolands showed up that evening literally bursting at the seams.

"Columbia University has made a special inquiry about en-rolling Carol this fall semester. I wanted to tell you Friday, but with the prom and everything I held back. I just could not wait until Monday. They have an accelerated program for outstanding students of Carol's caliber. I think it would be a superb opportunity for her. Columbia is one of the most outstanding universities in the country."

Margaret could see the lines deepening on Harold's fore-head. "Mr. Rolands," she began, "Carol is all we have. Naturally we want what is best for her. But, you under-stand, we will have to give this a lot of thought, and we will let you know of our decision by Monday."

"Well, okay." He seemed dejected.

"By the way, you must stay for dinner," she added cheer-fully.

Mr. Rolands perked up. "Now, Margaret, you know what I really came for." They all laughed heartily, fully breaking the stress. Margaret's Sunday night dinners were legendary. The local minister would come regularly. Dr. Chalmers was a frequent guest. With the recent passing of his wife, the only time he would really eat was when he was invited over.

The rest of the evening was a normal, cheerful night. Carol laughed with all of them. But she couldn't put the incident with Roger out of her mind. She still wasn't certain about what to do with her gown; she was just relieved that no one knew what had really happened...yet. Her forehead began to pound again.

CHAPTER 15
A PAINFUL DECISION

*A*fter a lot of discussion, and bold pressure from Margaret, Harold relented and informed Mr. Rolands they would accept Columbia's offer. Carol was advanced into the graduating class for that June.

She had managed to get every award imaginable at her school, as well as state recognition in the new rating exam—the Meniere Series. Her scores exceeded those of any of the students in the state.

In addition, Carol had excelled as a gymnast and had placed number one in the state's free form. It was only a lack of a rating system locally that kept her out of the national finals.

The last two months of school went by quickly. Carol occasionally would run into Roger on campus. They never spoke of that night. The prom dress was quietly packed up. Margaret never asked how the stain got on the dress...

As the class valedictorian that June, Carol stood in front of the parents as both an epitome of a young beauty and a scholar. Harold, Margaret, and Mrs. Praxton could not have been more proud. Almost all the citizens of Cedar Plains came to her graduation speech.

CHAPTER 16
THE DEPARTURE

The summer after graduation went too quickly. There was so much to do before Carol left—new clothes, books, course information. Plus the workload on the farm was increasing. New hands had to be hired. Harold was beginning to think about buying more land.

Evenings were mostly with family only. Occasionally Mr. Rolands would come over with new course information and the latest news about Columbia's programs. Everyone knew he really came over for Margaret's dinners.

Occasionally Dr. Chalmers would drop by—mostly to just visit. With the death of his wife, he felt himself aging more quickly and had tried to cut back his hours. He had hired two younger associates, much to his consternation.

"They just don't make 'em like they used to!" he said sourly. "Nowadays these younger bucks want to know how much they are going to make from the get-go. Plus all they can talk about is taking vacation. Whatever happened to quality care, continuity, and concern for the patient? It seems all they talk about is 'gimme, gimme, gimme.' I'm working more now than I ever have."

The sad truth was he was correct. With the influx of HMOs, government-funded health programs, and the like, a new breed of doctor was coming out—one that understandably wanted to be good in his profession, but now they wanted to have a life. The two didn't mix and never would. The simple fact was that in the real world, you get what you pay for. As medicine was getting more socialized and impersonal, the true quality of care was plummeting. Doctors spent little time with their patients. Instead, they felt just ordering more tests would fill the void...

Just as he was working everyone in a total state of depression talking about the decline in the quality of medicine, Margaret chimed in. "dessert is being served in the dining room!" Everyone instantly stood up and charged out, leaving the morose Dr. Chalmers to contemplate the facts that he knew to be all too true.

Despite the late evenings, everyone in the Lindsey household was up at dawn. Nothing had really changed. The chickens didn't bring their own eggs in or get their own feed on weekends. The cows hadn't learned how to milk themselves. The daily chores were unchanged.

Then the day came. Harold, Margaret, and Mrs. Praxton saw Carol off at the local bus stop. From there she would be going to Des Moines for the flight to New York.

For Harold, it was as though part of his life had ended.

"She belongs to the world, now, Harold," Margaret said. "It is out of our hands." She hugged him gently and wiped the tears off his cheeks.

CHAPTER 17
COLUMBIA UNIVERSITY

The campus at Columbia covered several acres—all well-kept brick buildings—sort of a mixture of Georgian and modern architecture, with an occasional hint of Frank Lloyd Wright.

It took Carol over an hour to find the girls' dormitory—a large, rather plain brick building in the corner of the campus. She entered, registered, and was given a room assignment. Along with this came a manual entitled *Guide to Appropriate Student Behavior for Women*.

She hauled all the belongings she had brought up to the door and inserted the key into the lock. The lock opened, but the door did not. She knocked.

"Just a minute!" came the sharp response.

Carol could hear a lot of shuffling and muffled voices. Eventually the door opened and a pleasant, petite girl stood there, almost panting. Her hair was sort of in disarray, and the two top buttons on her jeans were unbuttoned.

"You must be Carol Lindsey," she exclaimed. "I'm Dianne Merle, your roommate. You must forgive me...my boyfriend was helping me with my bags. Come here, Bill!" she ordered. Bill emerged from the bedroom. He also looked like he had dressed quickly. He greeted Carol with a sheepish grin. His pants were unzipped.

"Bill was just leaving," Dianne said with authority. With that, Bill disappeared down the hallway. "Come in! You must be tired from your trip. Do you have a preference for the right or left side of the bedroom?"

Carol looked around the small bedroom. One of the beds had been made up. A large pillow lay untouched at the head. The other looked like it had been hit by a tornado.

"I'm okay with that one," Carol said, pointing to the well-kept bed in the corner.

"Great!" Dianne smiled. "Let me help you unpack. Then we can tour the campus and find out where the cute guys hang out."

"I'm really here to study," Carol said. "Maybe we could go over to administration and check our course schedules," she volunteered.

"Okay," Dianne agreed. "But then we start scoping out the studs on campus."

Carol had never heard the word stud in reference to a guy. Where she came from, studs were used to support a fence.

"By the way," Dianne added, "feel free to throw that student manual in the trash. That's what I did with mine."

CHAPTER 18
THE CURRICULUM

Carol hit the ground running. Every course brought on a new challenge. Columbia was known for its accelerated programs and its combined graduate programs. At the beginning of her third year she was enrolled in the master's program in psychology at the Stein Institute.

After two years in a dormitory, Dianne convinced Carol to move to an apartment with her off campus.

"This stupid dormitory has a curfew that is very hard to work around," she would say. "If we had our own apartment, it would be no one's business when we came and went. Dormitory life just cramps my style…"

Dianne was a free spirit. Like Harold and Margaret, her parents were older but had given her a long leash. They were able to support her up to a point—but only for her part of the rent. Carol agreed to pay the other half from her scholarship fund. They would be on a tight budget, but she agreed to give it a try.

Dianne was pretty good as roommates go. She was a little messy, but a great companion when she was around. Once they were settled into the apartment she began to stay out much later. Some nights she never came home. She would call Carol on those nights—always with a good excuse. Apparently she was close to one of her aunts and would frequently spend the weekends with her—at least that was what she told Carol. That was fine with Carol. It just left her more time to study.

With the beginning of their senior year (actually, Carol was scheduled to graduate from the combined BA/master's program; Dianne was repeating several of the courses from her second- and third-year studies), Dianne came to Carol with distressing news.

"Carol, my parents just told me they are moving to Miami. Both my mom and dad are retiring, and they can barely pay my tuition for this year, let alone help me with living expenses."

Carol was already on a very tight budget. "Dianne, I don't think I can help...maybe we could move back on campus."

The very thought of moving back on campus made Dianne ill. "There just has to be another way." She pouted. "Wait! I just remembered—I just met a real nice guy—he's a little older, but he's a doctor and, up until now, has been a great friend. Maybe he has some ideas."

Carol had no idea what Dianne was thinking. However, over the next few months, Dianne always paid her half of the rent and seemed to have quite a bit left over for groceries and new clothes. Money issues never came up.

CHAPTER 19
GRADUATION

L ike so many events in Carol's life, graduation came all too quickly. Her parents made the trip from Iowa to New York in the old reliable pickup. They stayed in the apartment with her. Dianne was far from graduation. "I just need a few more credits," she would say. "I'll be staying with my aunt for the next few weeks, so your parents are welcome to stay."

The day itself was one of organized confusion. Over 1,200 students were being graduated in various disciplines—medicine, law, engineering, physics, psychology sciences… The entire campus was alive with excitement.

Again, her parents could not be more proud. She was among the first 75 students to complete the combined bachelor's/master's program from the Stein Institute. The dean had requested that applause be saved until all the 75 names were announced. However, when he read off the name Carol Lindsey, loud clapping came from the back of the audience. Carol wanted to die.

CHAPTER 20
NEW YORK

J ust before graduating, Carol landed a clerkship at the prestigious Bryan Institute for Psychological Studies. She would have to be there for one year to build up enough hours to take her boards for licensure. It included a modest stipend, but it meant Carol would have to move to upper Manhattan.

"Dianne," Carol said, after Dianne returned, "I have to move to be nearer the Bryan Institute."

"Carol!" Dianne beamed. "I'm starting my training as a court reporter just three blocks away from the Bryan Institute. You're not going to lose your roomie that easily. Besides, at Columbia they want me to study too much, and my parents can't cough up enough for another year's tuition. They think I am going to be a professional student."

They moved into a modest two-bedroom apartment in upper Manhattan. The move was relatively easy. For Carol it was mostly her books that required moving. For Dianne, it was her growing wardrobe.

Soon, they were settled and beginning their new careers. Dianne would still be gone for most of the weekends. For Carol, that just allowed her to prepare for the boards.

CHAPTER 21
"THE SOIREE"

Dianne's current boyfriend of the month was a clerk for one of the senior attorneys with Blakemore and Cohen. He had managed to get invited to one of their celebrated parties. These parties were primarily for the clients. It was also an opportunity for single women to meet successful attorneys and for men to meet attractive, younger ladies.

"You never get out," Dianne chided. "Men would kill for someone with a body like yours. It's about time you took the plunge. The worst thing that could happen would be you would enjoy yourself. You might even get laid!"

"Dianne!" Carol hissed, her cheeks burning. "Please don't talk that way."

Carol actually did come from a very conservative upbringing. With the exception of that one fateful event the night of the prom, she had never seen a man naked, let alone had any "contact."

"Carol, please," Dianne persisted. "We could go as a three-some. This guy I'm seeing is beginning to bore me."

"Dianne, it seems you get bored with all your guys."

"Well," Dianne said thoughtfully, "there is one you haven't met yet...I don't think I will ever get tired of him. Maybe I'll have him come over some evening."

"That would be nice, but for now, the boards are just six months away, and I need all my time to study."

"Carol! You aren't going to desert me in my time of need, are you?"

After seeing the exasperated look on Dianne's face, Carol conceded. "Allright! But let's have no more talk of getting l..." She could not even say the word. They both laughed.

"Carol," Dianne said, still laughing, "you have to realize that men are put on this earth to take care of you—both sexually and financially. You just have to train them in both aspects. And it is much better to have more than one to serve your needs. Some are better in the bedroom, and some are better in the financial end. Don't ever think you will find one man for both tasks."

"Dianne!" Carol gasped. "Let's just not go there again. I have agreed to go with you. Please, no more about your philosophy of men."

"Okay. But it's about time you got it in gear. You know what they say—use it or lose it..."

Carol just threw up her hands in desperation and retired to her bedroom to study.

CHAPTER 22
THE MEETING

The party was made up of the usual crowd—senior attorneys, new associates, some promising law students, and beautiful young ladies.

In the far corner, Carol saw a nice-looking young man staring at her. She averted her gaze. "Dianne," she whispered, "don't look, but who is that guy in the dark blue suit across the room?"

Dianne immediately turned around and fixed her eyes on the blue suit. He now had his back to them. "Omigosh!" she exclaimed, trying to muffle her voice. "That is John Berkowitz. Rumor around the courthouse is he is supposed to be the next partner with Blakemore and Cohen."

John Berkowitz was taller than most. He had dark hair, was clean-shaven and athletic. To Carol he stood out from all the others, but she tried to ignore him. He was surrounded by some of the office girls, who were obviously enjoying his company. Carol didn't know that some of his friends had already placed bets on who would be the first to get him into bed tonight.

Their meeting was quite coincidental. She had her back to him when someone accidentally fell toward her. She stepped back quickly but bumped into the drink John was holding, spilling it on him. "Oh my God!" she exclaimed. "Please excuse me! I'll be glad to pay for any cleaning or replacement."

His eyes pierced hers, if only for a moment; then he broke into a broad smile. "Don't worry about it. I have another Bernini exactly like this."

"At least let me get you another drink," she persisted.

"Please, let me do the honors." He beamed.

Without thinking, she followed him to the bar. She had forgotten about her friend. In fact, she had forgotten anyone else who was there. John was the only one she saw.

"I was just drinking club soda," she said shyly.

"Do you want to stay with that?" he asked.

"Please, I really don't drink."

The rest of the evening was like a dream. John was a great conversationalist. She learned he had done gymnastics in both high school and college.

"You really ought to come down here to Gold's Gym on the first floor. The partners didn't even want to rent any space to them, thinking they might attract the wrong crowd. I convinced them that would not be the case. Now, they have the most upscale members in Manhattan. Like us, they take up an entire floor, and it's rumored they want part of the second floor for their spa. The franchise owners gave me a life membership, and with the lease they signed, my partners think I walk on water."

As far as Carol was concerned, he did. In less than five minutes she had become totally enamored with him. She did not really notice that the conversation did center mostly on him; nor did she notice that he would look at himself every time he walked by a mirror.

The evening went very quickly. *Oh my goodness!* she thought to herself. *It's after midnight.* She had a full day of studying in front of her with the upcoming weekend. She started to formulate a sociably acceptable way to excuse herself.

"Wait," he said. "You aren't getting off that easy. I need your phone number in case my coat shrivels up from that drink."

The advance made her blush again. She hurriedly wrote her number on a napkin and handed it to him.

"I don't even know your last name," he said.

"Lindsey."

"Mine is Berkowitz," he said assertively. "Soon to be up there with Blakemore and Cohen-Berkowitz, Blakemore and Cohen, 'BBC.' I would assume they want it alphabetically."

"You seem very sure of yourself." She laughed.

"I am," he said firmly. "Wait! Let's start this right. I'm having dinner at Maxwell's tomorrow with my junior associates. It will be boring, but we can split off after an early dinner. Please join me."

"Really," she hesitated, "I have a board exam coming up soon and really have a lot of catching up to do."

"It will only be for a few hours," he protested. "I'll have you home early—I promise."

The offer was too good. "Okay. What time?"

"Meet me in the bar at six forty-five tomorrow night. Wear something ravishing."

The last statement took Carol aback. She wasn't accustomed to wearing the revealing outfits she saw on the other women. But she agreed she would be there 6:45 sharp.

CHAPTER 23
THE DATE

"O kay, Carol, this is the drill," Dianne began. "You have the body of a goddess, and it is a mortal sin not to let the male species appreciate this. Karma will catch up with you if you're not careful, and your body will wither up into an old prune."

They both laughed at this idea. Then Dianne produced three of her favorite evening dresses. She lately had acquired several evening dresses. Some were originals.

"Dianne! I can't wear any of these. They all look like nightgowns from Victoria's Secret."

"Carol!" Dianne chided. "This is your chance to enter the real world. This is what women wear to evening cocktail parties. This is what men want."

After much protesting and after going through many dresses, Carol picked the most conservative dress she could find. It was a beautiful dress by Scarpelli, one of New York's best designers. It had a flesh-colored material covered by a filigree overlay. At first glance it almost looked like she wasn't wearing anything. There was a split over the right leg coursing to her thigh.

"You can't wear anything under this," Dianne pointed out. "The lines will show through."

"Dianne..." Carol said in desperation. "I just can't!"

But after another hour of arguing, they finally compromised on a very unobtrusive undergarment.

This is no more than a G-string, Carol thought.

Nonetheless, Carol did look ravishing. And, by New York standards, the dress was moderately conservative. With each step her entire right leg was exposed.

The evening was wonderful. John was so dynamic and so energetic. They talked for hours—mostly about him. But she didn't care.

At the end of the night he kissed her passionately, several times. His kisses made her tremble all over. He made her feel things she had not felt since that night of the prom.

Their next time together was three days later. Again, it was perfect. John knew New York like the back of his hand. He treated her like a queen. She loved the attention. Each time he kissed her she could feel her body tingle all over.

CHAPTER 24
THE "TUTOR"

"For God's sake, Carol!" Dianne exclaimed. "You have gone out with this Adonis twice and you have only kissed him on the lips? You are going to lose him before you know it. The least you should do is…"

"Dianne!" Carol cut in, blushing a deep purple. "Please, you know I don't like that kind of talk."

Dianne had lived in New York for over five years. She had a very active sex life. She didn't even care if her partners were married. "The married guys are the safest," she would tell Carol. "And they can be very generous."

Carol never judged Dianne adversely. If Dianne was going to be out all night, she would always let Carol know. This happened a lot, but Carol figured that was her own business. And, besides, she enjoyed the solitude— it allowed her to study without being interrupted.

One evening the doorbell rang.

"Carol," Dianne yelled from the bathroom, "would you please get that? I think it's my date."

Carol opened the door to a pleasant-looking older man.

"Is Dianne ready?" he inquired.

"No, but she'll be out in a minute. Come in and have a seat. My name is Carol."

"Thank you," he replied warmly. "My name is Ken. Dianne is always late," he joked.

Carol felt obliged to sit with Ken. At first she felt a little awkward.

"What do you do for a living?" she asked.

"I'm a radiologist," he said matter-of-factly. "It's not a bad living, but the hours leave me little free time."

"Do you have children?" Carol asked. She suddenly realized she might have gotten too personal and she blushed.

"Oh, yes," Ken said, not missing a beat. "I have been married twice. I have a son and a daughter from each one. I just am not good at long-term relationships, I guess..." His voice seemed to trail off.

Some time elapsed while Dianne was readying herself, but Carol found Ken was easy to talk to. His considerate manner immediately put her at ease. For an older man he seemed to be in very good shape. Still—she wondered how old he was.

Soon, curiosity got the best of her. "How long have you been in practice?" she asked, ready to mentally add about 30 years to his answer.

Just then Dianne made her grand entrance. Her tight leather miniskirt accentuated her perfect thighs. Her breasts almost exploded over her bra. One of Ken's friends, probably the most notable plastic surgeon in New York, had done her implants—Ken's treat. She really looked like a knockout.

Carol didn't see Dianne until later the next day. But she just couldn't contain herself. "Dianne," she began cautiously, "is it okay if I ask you how old Ken is?"

"Sure," Dianne said cheerfully, "he just turned sixty-five."

"My God," Carol exclaimed. "He's eligible for Medicare. He's probably older than your father!"

"Only by two years. But he is the best lover I have ever known. If only I could get my boyfriend to do the things he does. And, besides, Ken is very generous, and he treats me like a princess."

"Is he married?" Carol asked cautiously.

"No, divorced for the last seven years. I gave up on married guys a long time ago—no future. Plus, he is really good in bed. Last night he…"

"Dianne!" Carol almost shouted. "Please spare me." She laughed. Dianne never ceased to amaze her. *Still*, she thought to herself, *he is nice to her, and maybe a little generosity isn't all that bad...*

CHAPTER 25
THE RELATIONSHIP

When Carol finally made love with John, there were none of the bells and whistles her friends had described. The act itself lasted less than 60 seconds and left her feeling very empty. She rationalized that it would get better. It would have to. After all, it was her first time and she had been very nervous. She was deeply in love with him.

They got into a routine of having sex on every date. There would be some foreplay; then John would get on top of her, and it would be over in a matter of seconds. She enjoyed feeling him inside her, but just when she was getting started, he was finished. *Maybe that is all there is to it*, she thought.

But something wasn't right.

At a weak moment she confided to Diane what had transpired. After all, this would be Dianne's field of expertise.

"Well," Dianne began very matter-of-factly, "you have to

get used to each other before you can both relax and enjoy yourselves."

This seemed logical to Carol.

"Let yourself explore his body, particularly below his waist. You know what I mean. That is the real way to a man's heart."

"No, Dianne, I'm not sure what you mean." The truth was that Carol didn't have a clue what Dianne was talking about.

"You mean you haven't tried going down on him? My boyfriend loves it, and the older guys think you're a goddess if you please them that way. It takes getting used to—but men love this. It's even better when they return the favor. In fact, it's the only way I have a real orgasm. Men need to be taught what really excites you. You can teach them if you are in control—and if you master oral sex, you will have ultimate control. Men will swoon at your feet."

Carol didn't really know what an orgasm was. She had learned to "stimulate" herself at an early age, but had never had anyone else do this to her. She didn't want to "control" John; she just wanted to feel some of the excitement Dianne always talked about, and more than anything, she wanted to please him. And the idea of having John swoon at her feet wasn't all that bad.

"It's really just a matter of practice, Carol."

Carol realized this was the real voice of experience. You wouldn't find this in any sex manual.

"And practice starts now, Carol!" Dianne sounded as

though she were teaching a class. She trimmed the tip off a ripe banana and slowly worked almost the entire length of it into her mouth. She rinsed it and handed it to Carol.

"Now, you try it!"

As usual Carol blushed. Anytime the discussion was about sex, Dianne made Carol blush.

"Dianne..I..- maybe I'll just wait for the right time."

Taken out of context, the whole idea seemed unreal to Carol, but when she felt the time was right, she did "go down" on John. She tried to do everything just as Dianne had outlined.

He lay back, moaning softly. Carol now knew what Dianne meant by being in control. She enjoyed giving him this pleasure. Again, it was over quickly. It was a bit of a shock to her, but she enjoyed pleasing him.

He never tried to "return the favor." In fact, he would barely touch her below the waist. Carol was extremely hygienic. However, like so many women, she had been programmed to think that area was "unclean," and if John didn't want to go there, it was okay. She enjoyed pleasing him and found it excited her a bit.

When she told her roommate how things were going, Dianne was flabbergasted.

"Good heavens, Carol! What have I been telling you? Men have to be trained. Just grab the back of his head and throw a leg lock around his neck. He'll get the idea. And don't let him come up for air until you are satisfied." Dianne lay back on the bed, grabbed a pillow, and pretended it was a guy's head.

Carol was aghast. "Dianne, you can't just do that. Maybe the guy just doesn't like to do that." But the sight of Dianne on the bed with a pillow stuffed between her legs made them laugh uncontrollably.

"Here," Dianne said. "It's your turn." She threw the pillow at Carol.

More laughter. Carol's sides hurt.

"But Carol," Dianne finally added seriously, "if you don't teach them from the get-go, it might not get any better. Don't rely on time to improve things. Especially when it comes to sex."

CHAPTER 26
THE PROPOSAL

But their lovemaking didn't really change much. Carol didn't have the nerve to use John's head as Dianne had shown her. She was just content that she was satisfying him. She was certain that it would get better. To heck with what Dianne had to say.

They had only been dating now for about three months. And despite the fact there had been no real change in their lovemaking, she was convinced he was the only man for her. His kisses still set her on fire, and she enjoyed pleasing him.

One warm, actually humid night, Carol and John were having dinner at Bertolli's—one of the five-star restaurants New York is so famous for. Bertolli's was located on the top of the Crowler building, and on warm nights, they could roll back the roof and people would dine under full view of the Manhattan skyline.

She hadn't seen him for an entire week. He had been upstate on a case, or so he had said. Each day without him seemed like an inquisition. Dianne had tried to get her out, but Carol wouldn't budge.

"You really have got to get out, Carol. No matter how much you like one flavor of ice cream, there are at least thirty-one more."

"I'm just not interested, Dianne." Carol blushed.

This time it was Dianne who threw up her hands. "Fine!" she exclaimed. "…just more for me."

She had missed him desperately. But here they were under the stars. A light, warm breeze ruffled his hair. She couldn't take her eyes off him.

"Carol," he began, gently grasping her hand, "the firm I am with is really into traditional family values. All the partners are married. The wives stay home and raise the children. That is just an unwritten rule." He began to stutter. "C- C- Carol, I want you to become my wife—Mrs. Berkowitz. You won't have to finish your internship or worry about board exams. I will take care of you always. You won't ever have to work."

The thought of not pursuing her career or fulfilling her dreams stopped her for a moment. She was only two months from completing her clerkship. But a marriage to such a highly successful attorney whose income would dwarf anything she could make would be a very good and logical substitute. She knew she was rationalizing. But at the same time, she did not want to risk losing him.

Without hesitating she said yes. She gazed into his dark eyes. She knew what she was doing was the absolute right thing. Maybe, if she wanted to do so, she could someday finish her internship and take her boards. For now it just didn't seem relevant. Only her future life with John had any meaning.

They planned a June wedding. Carol's father insisted on paying for this, but John's tastes were off the board. John gave Carol the money for the expense overruns.

It was a beautiful wedding. John's parents were Episcopalian, although he had been in a church only twice in his life. This was the second time. Carol's parents, on the other hand, were Methodist. But because there were few Methodist churches in New York proper, they relented. "After all, we have a Protestant background," Margaret would say.

Dianne was the maid of honor. She was not thrilled with the dress she had to wear. "Carol," she protested, "this is just like what the Muslim men make their women wear." But since Carol was really her best friend, she relented. She did bring Ken as her escort, however, and that did raise a few eyebrows. But her relationship with her current boyfriend was in a rut. He was way too possessive and was soon to be dumped. She had lately found herself being more and more drawn to Ken, in spite of his age.

As Carol's father stood by the altar, she saw, for the second time, big tears running down his cheeks. She hugged him when she reached the altar. "You will always be my little girl," he sobbed.

The reception was in the main ballroom at the Waldorf. John had prepaid for a suite for Carol's parents and insisted she convince them it was only $100 per night. The suite came with a large Jacuzzi tub and a bidet. "I could go for a swim in that tub," her father said. "And that other thing…I turned that on and got hit square in the face. The water shoots clear up to the ceiling. I don't even want to know what that is for…"

CHAPTER 27
MARRIAGE

The first few months with John were wonderful. She seemed to be the center of his attention. His practice was going well, and he was generally home by 5 p.m.

Shortly after his marriage, John was brought in as a full partner. The firm liked the idea of placing their names alphabetically – Berkowitz, Blakemore & Cohen—BBC.

Carol had joined Gold's Gym on the first floor of the firm's building. When John was in the office, they would have lunch together. She enjoyed keeping herself in good shape. Secretly she was very proud of her figure.

Their love life continued to be one-sided, however. John had coined a word for the way he liked to be pleased by calling it "TLC." They would go to bed, he would kiss her briefly, and then ask for "TLC." When he was satisfied, he would kiss her on the forehead, roll over, and go to sleep.

CHAPTER 28
BANKRUPTCY

Harold and Margaret had used their life savings to send Carol to Columbia. Having lived all their lives in Iowa, they thought of New York as the center of the universe. The only thing they did get right was the college. It had a very progressive humanities department. The reputation of the psychology department was second to none.

The early 1990s saw the demise of many family-owned farms. There were years of drought followed by relentless floods.

Carol's parents were among those who had assumed a heavy debt in the 1990s to expand. The notes were now coming due. With the destruction of so much of their land and the loss of their crops, there was no income. There would be no extensions or renegotiations with the bank.

When her parents finally told her of the impending bankruptcy, Carol was frantic. "Mom, why didn't you tell me sooner?"

"We didn't want to bother you, honey. You had just married that fancy lawyer, and we just didn't want to complicate things. You and John are just starting your lives together."

"I'll tell John," Carol said firmly. "He will know how to handle this."

When she told John about her parents' dilemma, she saw, for the first time, a side of him she disliked. "Farms are a losing business, sweetheart," he began very matter-of-factly. "It's like throwing your money down a big hole. We would never see a cent on our return."

John's cold cruelty was starting to surface. Carol never brought the subject up again. There was no point.

Her family's farm was sold by the bank at a bankruptcy auction. This was becoming a very familiar scene in the Midwest.

About the only object that did not sell was a dilapidated house trailer behind the barn. Her grandparents had originally lived in it until they had completed their home. Her dad put on some newer tires and managed to drag it to a local trailer park, the final "end" for so many farming families. There her dad tried to squeeze out a living selling firewood.

The call came around 1 a.m.

"Mrs. Berkowitz?" a strange voice asked.

"Yes," Carol replied. "Why are you calling in the middle of the night?"

"I'm Lieutenant Thompson of the Cedar Plains PD. Are your parents Harold and Margaret Lindsey?"

"Yes," Carol replied; her head began to pound.

"I'm afraid I have some bad news for you," the voice continued.

Carol's throat tightened.

"Your parents were found in their trailer today by a neighbor. They were heating it with an old heater—carbon monoxide poisoning." The voice was very matter-of-fact.

"Are they going to be okay?" Carol cried. She refused to believe what she was hearing.

"Mrs. Berkowitz, I'm trying to tell you your parents are dead."

Carol dropped the phone and fell to the bed silently. The jolt from her hitting the bed awoke John.

"Sweetheart! What's the matter?"

She sobbed uncontrollably, telling him the story. It was only much later she realized the man trying to console her was the one who could have made the difference.

In a few weeks, life returned to "normal." A part of her had learned to resent John wholeheartedly—a part she couldn't face for now.

Her parents actually did have some assets. After the federal, state, and county took their cut, Carol actually did receive about $10,000. The check had come to her in her maiden name. Carol looked at the check dispassionately. *A generation of blood and sweat for $10,000...* she thought.

Carol never told John about the check—she just opened an account and let the money sit. She didn't know just why she did things this way—she might have thought she would surprise him once it accumulated enough interest.

CHAPTER 29
PREGNANCY

O nce things became somewhat normal, their sex life resumed. Carol was thrilled when she announced to John she was pregnant.

"I thought you were taking precautions," he had said.

Again, her feelings of resentment toward him resurfaced. Still, she could not face reality.

Once she began to show, he seemed to want "TLC" more frequently. She would always accommodate him as a dutiful wife. Morning sickness was no excuse. However, she was noticing a change. Sex gradually became an unpleasant reality. It was no different than her regular household duties. She stopped feeling any excitement and simply would emotionally separate herself from what she was doing. Still, she counted her blessings as being the wife of a successful lawyer with a good future ahead of him. *Things will get better after the baby is born,* she would think.

At the office parties, she noticed how the secretaries would look at him. She wasn't the jealous or suspicious type, however, and she simply passed it off. Infidelity on John's part was unthinkable.

As Carol entered her third trimester, John's attitude became more offensive. He told her he didn't see how she could ever get back to her original weight of 102. She knew better, but the comments still hurt. From her gymnastics in high school she knew what it was like to really work out. Her instructor then had given birth to three boys. She was 38, but she had a sculptured figure that guys could not help notice. "You can do an awful lot with regular exercise," she would tell her students. "Just because you have three kids, you don't have to look like it." Carol kept that thought as her goal.

The late nights became more frequent. At first John would manage to call. "Another late one," he would say flatly. "Don't bother waiting up for me."

But Carol would wait up.

After the birth of a beautiful baby boy, Jason, John seemed to become warmer toward her. Sex, as it was, however, mostly centered around satisfying him. Occasionally, he would pat the top of her head when it was over and mumble how good she was. That made her feel like a faithful dog. After he was "satiated," he would just roll over and go to sleep. That made her feel worse. Kissing was a thing of the past.

After eight weeks, her episiotomy had completely healed and she felt she was ready to resume normal sex. However, when he got on top of her, he complained it was different, less stimulating. This really hurt her. She vowed to herself that she was going to get into such good shape that he would have nothing to complain about.

Unfortunately, she began to realize that mutually pleasing sex was going to be nonexistent. *Well,* she thought, *it was never that good for me to start with...maybe I am just that way.*

As the late nights became more frequent, the phone calls ceased. She had to guess when he would be coming home. But she did have her hands full with Jason. *John never bothered to even try to change a diaper,* she mused to herself.

Jason was a beautiful little boy. All her time would be devoted to him.

When he was six months old, she decided to finish the rest of her hours and take her boards. She had arranged for a part-time housekeeper from the meager allowance John gave her, and she would only be gone two nights a week until 9 p.m. Since he frequently was gone until then, she didn't think this would affect things.

"You are turning your back on our son just to get a stupid counseling certificate that you'll never use," he exclaimed.

"And you are letting your work take you away from both of us," Carol retorted. It was about the first time she had dared to talk back.

"Well, someone has to make the money; you sure as hell would never be able to support us. Not unless you want us to live in a house trailer."

She hated confrontations with John. The last statement was

particularly cruel since her beloved parents had died in a house trailer. His reaction to any confrontation hurt her deeply. She was starting to wonder if he really cared. She began to take one day at a time. What she thought was her dream marriage was now becoming a nightmare.

Despite John's negative comments, Carol was able to finish all her hours as well as take the boards. She was satisfied to get her certificate by mail and intended to activate her license as soon as possible.

One night he called and explained, somewhat coldly, that he would be gone for the weekend. A new client had signed on with them, and he would be in Connecticut for the weekend. The explanation seemed reasonable and she simply accepted it. She actually shocked herself when she faced the realization that she did not mind his being gone.

CHAPTER 30
THE SEPARATION

In spite of their souring relationship, Carol was shocked when John suggested they try a "trial" separation.

"You've changed, Carol," he said dispassionately. "You only seem concerned about Jason and setting up your practice to deal with a bunch of neurotic New York psychos."

Despite her pleas to the contrary, he told her he felt she did not want him around and that they had to live apart to "sort things out."

Still in shock, she packed a few things quickly for herself and Jason and drove away in her BMW. She did not know where to turn—then she remembered Dianne.

Dianne had moved to a spacious apartment in the trendy section of Manhattan. On a recent visit there, Carol had been incredulous. "How can you afford this? Do court reporters really make that much?" Dianne told her that her parents had left her a trust that helped her make ends meet. Carol never asked for details.

Now, Carol turned to the only one she felt was her true friend. *Please be home,* Carol thought.

Dianne did happen to be home. Upon hearing the plight of her best friend, her first comment was, "I always took him for a pig! Carol, I'm sorry, but there are just guys like that—they can't be trained. You and Jason are welcome to stay as long as you like. I have two extra bedrooms. Besides," she went on, "I've been seeing a lot more of Ken lately. He wants to take me to this mysterious Caribbean island near the Grand Caymans—Berneau or something like that. I think he wants me to marry him. I could do worse. And this court reporter stuff really sucks!"

John would call occasionally—mostly to inquire about Jason. He had not changed anything in their joint account or in their credit cards. She still drove her new BMW. She took all this as a sign that they would be back together soon.

Still, she had started feeling much better about herself since they had separated. She was able to spend more time at the gym and was back to her original weight. Her body was toned, and she felt she was every bit as good as when she was 17.

In addition, she was now actively setting up her practice as a marital counselor. Who better to do marital counseling than someone from a failing relationship? But she was certain they would get back together.

John would invite her back to "their" house on occasion on the pretext of seeing Jason. The real reason would be to have sex with her in the way to which he was accustomed—after Jason went to sleep. She always obliged him, regardless of what she was starting to feel. It really wasn't sex to her anymore, but just something she had become accustomed to.

Over the last few weeks, he seemed to be warming up to her more. He had invited her over three nights last week and was actually affectionate with her after she had "taken care" of him. He even let her stay over. She felt certain he would soon be asking her to move back in—maybe he just needed "a push."

She had set aside 30 minutes daily for a very hard workout at the gym. When alone at home, she would inspect herself carefully. She was proud of the way she looked, and she desperately wanted to make John take notice. She also had become familiar with Kegel exercises and would go through them constantly every night and at any opportunity during the day. She could squeeze her smallest finger until it hurt. She thought this would please him.

When Carol didn't hear from John by Saturday, she decided to pack up Jason and pay a surprise visit. After all, he was still her husband. He was probably preoccupied with some ongoing case.

She decided to be a little daring and dressed in the black leather miniskirt Dianne had loaned her. She topped that with a sheer blouse. She looked fantastic! How could he be disappointed? In addition she had just bought a completely transparent negligee from Frederick's. *This will get his attention,* she thought confidently.

On the way over to their house, she decided she would cut back her practice to part-time. She had been reviewing a Health Maintenance Organization (HMO) contract that seemed very good. This HMO was anxious to set up relationships with paramedical personnel to expand their scope of benefits. This would have to take a backseat for the time being, however.

It was a cold March Saturday afternoon. John's car partially blocked the driveway, and Carol had to park down the street. On the walk back to the house, the cold air actually made her nipples more obvious through her blouse. It just made her that much more desirable. She had rarely felt so good about herself.

She unlocked the door and came in—Jason in one arm and an overnight bag in another. The first thing she noticed was the smell of perfume—not hers. She leaned around the corner in the anteroom, and there, lying on the couch, was a willowy blonde in the same see-through negligee she had just bought from Frederick's.

"Hello," Carol said pleasantly. "And who might you be?" As she arose, Carol could see that the negligee left nothing to the imagination. *She's not even a real blonde*, she thought.

Just then John came in the room with two glasses of wine. He was totally taken by surprise. "Carol! What are you doing here?"

Carol just stood there. In less than an instant, any feeling she ever had for this man completely evaporated. The real nature of their relationship for the last year replayed through her mind in a matter of seconds. She was asking herself the classic question: how could she have been so stupid?

"I'm your wife, you bastard!" she said. Her eyes blazed at him. She could feel herself blush all over. Jason began to whimper.

John just stood there nonchalantly sipping from his glass.

The blond "guest" tried to break the ice. "John, darling!" she said. "You never told me you had such a cute little boy." She glided over to give Jason a hug.

"Touch him, bitch, and you die," Carol hissed.

The blonde froze in her tracks. *She can't be more than nineteen*, Carol thought.

"Carol!" John exclaimed. "I didn't know you were capable of using such filthy language."

"The truth is, you narcissistic, self-centered, slimy bastard, is that you don't really know what I am capable of." All Carol saw was red. She grabbed Jason and left, leaving her overnight bag with the Frederick's negligee behind.

She knew her threats to John were empty, but she wanted to make him uncomfortable.

CHAPTER 31
DIVORCE

R eality set in quickly. John liquidated their joint account and cancelled her credit cards. She was able to obtain a new Mastercard, but the credit line was small and expensive. Her lawyer assured her that they would get an ample settlement from John. He only required a $10,000 retainer to cover upfront expenses.

"What expenses?" Carol asked. "Don't you just serve him or something?" She realized she knew nothing about the legal system, but just assumed that John would have to split their joint account and provide some child support before a settlement was reached.

"Carol," her attorney began gently, "John is a partner with a very powerful law firm, with high-powered divorce attorneys. They will do everything to protect him. He is an investment for them. The ten thousand will barely cover what I will have to pay an accountant to assess his assets and subpoena a K-1 from the firm. I'll probably need a little extra later to cover any overruns, but that can wait until after the settlement."

Carol thought about what her parents had left her. The total amount of money they had to show for their entire lifetime of hard labor was $10,000. She was now signing that over on one piece of paper.

The next day she went out to her car in time to see it being driven away. A nervous young man in a tailored suit handed her a repossession summons. The firm of Berkowitz, Blakemore and Cohen was repossessing her BMW. It turned out that the firm leased all the partners' cars, and they kept extra keys.

"There is nothing I can do," her lawyer protested. "Most large firms lease exotic automobiles for their partners. The car essentially belongs to the corporation, and they can do with it as they please. Furthermore," he went on, "they have quashed my request for financial records regarding any income or assets received by John. It will be three or four months before we get a hearing. They are refusing to settle on any request, claiming infidelity on your part."

"Infidelity," she yelled. "Who the hell do you think he was carrying on with in our own home?" She was shaking, she was so mad.

"Carol, calm down," her attorney said reassuringly. "We will get a hearing, and a settlement figure will be negotiated at that time. Rome wasn't built in a day, you know."

"And what can I do in the meantime?" she said, now feeling exasperated. "I'm already living on borrowed money."

"All we can do is wait for the hearing. Oh!" he added. "I will need a little more expense money. This firm will be a tough nut to crack. I may need more money soon."

The divorce would be "arbitrated" by a retired judge. This was frequently done to minimize court costs. Carol's attorney soon realized he could get little from her and was anxious to bring this to a close. The hearing was in a small office, just two blocks down from the BBC Building. It was attended by Carol, her attorney, and Mr. Blakemore himself—appearing on behalf of John and the firm. John did not attend. His presence was not required.

The hearing got off to an explosive start with an opening salvo from John's attorney. "Your Honor," Mr. Blakemore began coldly, "Mr. Berkowitz has provided DNA evidence that Jason is not his child. This is irrefutable."

"Mr. Blakemore," the judge said equally coldly, "I will decide what evidence is irrefutable."

Carol sat, dumbfounded, not knowing how to respond. Even her own attorney looked scornfully at her.

"It seems that the last time Mr. Berkowitz took Jason in for a haircut, he sent out a lock of hair for DNA analysis. This shows clearly that Jason could not be his son. The hair was submitted by Mr. Bernado. We would like to introduce this as 'Exhibit One.'" He thrust the paper at the judge.

Carol knew Mr. Bernado. He was a kind, heavyset man who was the exclusive hair stylist for BBC. He had even done her hair on a few occasions. The firm was his sole source of income.

"Judge," Carol's attorney interjected, "could I please have a word with my client?"

"Of course," the judge said. "We can have a brief recess."

Carol's attorney ushered her into a small room behind the office.

"Carol," he began, "you never raised the possibility that Jason could have another father."

"It just can't be," Carol protested. "It is really impossible." Her mind was spinning, and her head began to hurt worse than ever.

"I'm sorry, Carol. I have no grounds to contest irrefutable evidence."

The hearing was over that day. Carol was not to receive any alimony. Mr. Berkowitz had volunteered to provide $10,000 for a one-time payment plus $250 a month in child support, just as a matter of "goodwill." If this were to be contested, the offer would be withdrawn.

"I feel, under the circumstances, this is the best you can do," her attorney informed her. "Another five thousand will barely cover my additional expenses."

CHAPTER 32
MAURY

I n a few months, Carol had learned to assume the role of a single working mother. With the settlement, she had paid for the first six months of Jason's preschool and had opened a small office in Queens. She managed to get a business startup loan from her S&L at 16%. She also managed to finance a used Honda, also with the same S&L at the same interest rate. "Once you get established, we can renegotiate the terms," the bank official told her matter-of-factly.

Carol had signed on with a very large HMO and was already getting several referrals. She was also seeing some patients with Medicaid coverage. She felt it was only a matter of time until she would be making a good income.

One of her early referrals would prove to be the turning point of her career. This was Kathleen and Maury Lenowitz.

Maury Lenowitz was short, fat, and unattractive. Tying his own shoes was his major source of exercise. Heavy glasses with Coke bottle lenses dwarfed his pudgy face.

Kathleen, Maury's wife, was also heavyset, although not to the degree Maury was. She was tall, unattractive, and wore way too much makeup. She towered over Maury. And she dominated him. Carol watched them as they entered the room. Maury walked hunched over behind Kathleen, who dragged him in by the hand and ordered him to sit in a chair separate from her.

Before Carol could even begin the basic interview, Kathleen cut in.

"He's a pig," she blurted out. "A real sicko."

Maury just sat there, totally dejected.

After some probing, Carol learned what had really occurred—Kathleen had caught him masturbating. She looked upon this as a gross act of infidelity. She wanted him punished. She didn't mention that sexual contact with her short, fat, timid husband was almost nonexistent.

Their problems centering on lack of intimacy were not unusual. Her HMO referred her many similar cases. This came through a family practitioner or "gatekeeper" in the new medical language of the 1990s. Rarely, they came as direct referrals from attorneys who wanted to prolong the divorce to make more money. Anyone knows that the best way to prolong a divorce is to order marital counseling. The attorneys paid for these sessions up front. There was no delay in payment. This was the only thing that attorneys did right. They, in turn, made three to four times what they would normally make on a divorce settlement. Unfortunately, less than 5% of her practice was attorney referrals.

Attorneys had become a real curiosity to Carol. They truly had no concept of ethics or decency. Their only concern was to give their client the best representation money could buy and make as much money as possible. If the client could not consistently pay their fees, the degree of representation would decline. If their client ran out of money, they would be referred to legal aid.

Despite the fact the HMO had not paid her a cent, Carol put a good deal of her energy into trying to counsel Maury and Kathleen. Maury was receptive to her suggestions; Kathleen, however, was very negative. The sessions were not going well.

CHAPTER 33
THE HMO

C arol started out with a very negative cash flow, which worsened quickly over time. The health maintenance organizations, or HMOs, were springing up all over the country as a solution to rapidly rising medical costs. They would come in a variety of corporate structures. They all had the same theme, however. The HMOs would come to those individuals such as Carol and offer to provide them with a heavy case load, in return for which they would want them to charge less. In addition, the HMO would require a prodigious amount of paperwork. Reimbursement would generally be delayed or denied over the most minor clerical errors. There were grandiose promises of "reorganization and restructuring," with future payments just around the corner. However, these were further ploys to get the "health provider" to continue to see the HMO patients. The ongoing theme with the HMO was to delay or deny payment as frequently as possible. In the meantime they would collect the monthly payments from the enrollees and reap huge profits from the interest in the corporate investments. It was the closest thing to organized crime, and it was fully sanctioned by federal and state agencies. In addition, declara-

tion of bankruptcy was a favorite maneuver by these organizations in order to avoid making payouts to the health
care providers. Just before bankruptcy would be declared,
all the executives comprising the upper echelon of the
HMO would receive seven-figure bonuses and move on to
restructuring. Not even the Mafia could pull these maneu-
vers.

Any legal recourse by the health provider was frustrating
and costly. Very few attorneys would represent a healthcare
provider who was pushed to the brink of bankruptcy by an
HMO. The average provider was left with nothing. The ac-
tual money would end up in the hands of a few enterprising
doctors, administrators, and businessmen—all of whom,
like attorneys, had no concept of decency or ethics.

The federal and state "health" plans were equally frustrating. Here Carol would spend hours filling out forms for
every couple she saw. Payment was always delayed, if not
totally denied because of some meaningless oversight in the
paperwork. The people administering all these plans had
the equivalent of a third-grade education and no ability to
think cognitively.

After 12 months of promises and little income, Carol was
looking at huge debts. Fortunately, Dianne was on an ex-
tended vacation with Ken. "Carol, I really mean it—you
can stay as long as you wish!" she had said before she left.

However, Carol was six months behind in her office rent.
The bank was ready to call in the business startup loan because of nonpayment. Furthermore, they were going to re-
possess her used Honda Civic as soon as they could hire a
car thief sleazy enough to "steal" it. Finally, Jason's preschool was letting her know on a daily basis that she was
four months behind in his tuition.

CHAPTER 34
THE PROPOSITION

O ver the last several weeks, Carol had seen Maury becoming more and more depressed. Kathleen dominated the visits to the point that Carol would almost lose control of the session. This large, overbearing lady would use the session to embarrass and deride her husband. She repeatedly made him confess to his episode of "infidelity."

He had defensively announced that his solo accounting business was growing by leaps and bounds. Carol did notice the new diamonds Kathleen wore, as well as the red fox fur from Dejone on their last visit. The influx of such significant amounts of money had no effect on their relationship, however. It was simply not enough. It was never enough. And it would never be enough. This pitiful little man would never have any level of affection unless he succumbed to one of the girls who walked the streets on 7th Avenue. And if that ever happened, he knew Kathleen would leave him since he would immediately get AIDS. At least he was convinced that was the case.

With her limited experience as a counselor, Carol could see no real way to help Maury. He sank deeper and deeper into depression.

For this particular session, Maury had shown up alone.

"Kathleen had to get her nails done," he began. "This was the only time she could go."

It was interesting to Carol that a nail appointment would supersede a session devoted to improving one's marriage. But it was not surprising. Kathleen just wanted Maury's financial support. He had nothing else to offer her. At least nothing she really wanted.

So, here she was sitting alone in her soon to be foreclosed office with a decent, very depressed, fat little man.

"I have nothing!" he sobbed.

"Nonsense," said Carol encouragingly. "You have one of the most successful accountancy practices in Manhattan. You said so yourself."

"Yes," he sobbed, "but that isn't enough for my wife. We haven't had any type of intimate contact for months. She doesn't want me to touch her. She calls me a repulsive dwarf."

He buried his head in his hands. His body shook unevenly with his sobs.

"Maury," Carol began, "you are a kind, decent man. You are successful. Let's try to get Kathleen to come with you later on this week."

She felt so uneasy with Maury. She wanted so desperately to help him, but at the same time, she just wanted him and the entire situation to go away.

"I have read that sometimes you can recommend a surrogate in these situations," he said between sobs.

"Maury," she said as gently as she could, "that isn't done in this day and age. The results with sexual surrogates are very controversial, and the concept borders on prostitution."

"I know," he said quietly. "But I have no options left for me." He tried to look at her, but could not. He then began timidly, "Would you ever consider helping me with this problem?"

At this point Carol was aghast. She felt herself taking on the role of Kathleen. She looked at him with disdain. "Under no circumstances could I even consider this," she said harshly.

"Please," he begged softly. "Money is no object. I would give ten thousand dollars just to be with you. I have read about professional surrogates, and this is the only way I can see for me. Kathleen and I haven't had sex since our honeymoon... The money really means nothing to me."

Carol's mind went numb. It was then she realized she had mentally spent most of the $10,000 to just break even for the month.

"I could never consider this," she said firmly. "I'm afraid we will have to terminate our sessions."

"NO!" he exclaimed. "You are my last hope." He began to

sob uncontrollably. Carol could hear the desperation in his voice and knew for a fact that he was suicidal at this point. "I could pay you in cash," he added. "I handle huge sums of money for my clients, most in cash. I have ten thousand dollars in hundreds with me in this envelope." He produced a thick brown envelope and practically handed it to her.

Again, her mind went numb. To her horror, a little voice inside her was telling her to do it. The money would solve all her problems. She had run through every possible scenario in her mind. Facing bankruptcy, she felt she had very limited options. She remembered how her parents had lost their farm in bankruptcy court, how they both died shortly thereafter. She thought of Jason...

Carol looked at the little man sitting there, his body shaking with each sob. She realized some quirk of fate had put them in this situation. She desperately needed money, and he desperately needed feminine contact.

"Okay," she heard herself say quietly.

She excused herself, went to the bathroom, and returned wrapped in a towel. She handed an extra towel to Maury. In less than an instant he had disrobed and wrapped the towel around his waist. His fat quivered over the edges of the towel.

"Lie down on the couch," Carol said quietly, trying to detach herself from what she was about to do. She unwrapped the towel around him. All she could see below his waist were rolls of fat. Fortunately, he had immaculate hygiene. She could smell his cologne. It was the same John had used.

"Put this on." She handed him a condom. Closing her eyes,

she gradually lowered herself on top of him. She couldn't even tell if he was really inside her. There was no feeling.

She carefully balanced herself on top of him and began to move up and down slowly. She could hear him moaning softly. She had never heard such noises.

In less than 20 seconds, she noticed his body was shaking uncontrollably. He let out a loud yelp that echoed in her ear—it was over!

Trying to ignore the loud ringing in her right ear, she slipped off him as quickly as she could and almost ran to her bathroom. Out of the corner of her eye, she could see him lying there, gasping for breath.

After a quick, almost scalding shower, she came back in the room to see him lying on the couch, motionless. The towel covered him loosely.

My God! she thought. *He's had a heart attack!* How could she ever explain this? She knew she would have to finish dressing him before calling 911. But with a heart attack, didn't every second count? And what could she tell the police? She knew she was a lousy liar. A simple autopsy would probably show exactly what had just transpired. An investigation would reveal everything. Should she try CPR?

The towels, she thought. *I must get rid of them.*

Her mind was racing. Nothing was making sense. She was certain her career was over and she would be spending the rest of her life at Attica. She thought of Jason and what would become of him. She would never see him again. Her head began to pound.

Just as she was dialing 911, she noticed him move. He was sobbing quietly.

Carol breathed a sigh of relief. Her mind quickly tried to bring her to a normal level of rationality.

"Nobody has ever given me such a wonderful experience," he sobbed. "I will never be able to thank you enough."

"Finish dressing," she said. She wanted him to cover himself so she didn't have to look at him. In fact, she did not wish to see him ever again.

Obediently, he dressed quickly. As he left he tried to say something, but Carol waived him out. She sat there, not knowing what to do. The brown envelope lay on the table.

"Well, you might as well take the money," a little voice said inside her. "After all, you earned it. In less than thirty seconds you made more than your parents had saved in their lifetime."

She did pick up the envelope. She also resolved never to see Maury or Kathleen again. She would refer them to another provider.

CHAPTER 35
RELIEF

"**M**s. Berkowitz," the voice began sternly, "our principal, Mr. Rohrer, wanted me to remind you again that you are over four months behind on Jason's tuition. It would be a shame if we had to..." The voice trailed off. Ms. Starron had initially been so gracious to Carol when she first enrolled Jason in their preschool. Carol had paid for the first three months in advance. That had been over seven months ago. Now, Ms. Starron glared at her coldly, as if getting some pleasure out of being Mr. Rohrer's messenger.

"I cashed a check this morning and have the money with me," Carol said, trying to control herself. This woman really made her sick.

"Well, in that case, let me take you to the office and get a receipt. I am so glad that Jason can stay on with us. He is such a talented little man!"

The rest of the money went to the back rent for her office and to bring the payments on her business loan up to date.

The lease on her Honda was also paid. She had $335 left over. That all went to new clothes for Jason.

CHAPTER 36
THE DILEMMA

L ater that next week, Maury showed up unannounced. Carol was in between clients and agreed to see him. She had already decided what she was going to say.

"No, Maury!" she said sternly. "I can never do that again. It is imperative that you and Kathleen go to counseling together. I am referring you to another therapist." She realized what she had just said was ludicrous. No therapist could deal with Maury and Kathleen as a couple—let alone have sex with him.

He fell back, dejected. He then sank to his knees in front of her.

"Please," he begged. "You have given me something to live for. I don't have anything else. The money means nothing to me. It's just paper. I can transfer twenty thousand dollars a week to an offshore account in your name, and no one would know the difference. Offshore banking is my specialty. The IRS has no authority to deal with the offshore corporations I have set up."

Again, Carol felt her mind spinning out of control. That little voice inside her kept saying, "Come on, Carol. You did it once. What's the problem? The first time was only twenty seconds, and you just got offered a one hundred percent raise…"

"Maury," she began quietly, "I just can't. It is so unethical and goes against all my principles."

"Please," he pressed. "I have nothing…nowhere to turn."

Again she heard that little voice within her. "Just say yes! After one month you can do anything you want! Don't try to think—just do it!"

She felt herself nodding quietly.

"You've no idea what you have done for me!" He beamed. "I'll see you Friday."

He left through the patient exit. She actually saw a smile on his face for the first time.

Carol sat quietly in her chair. She wasn't sure what to think. Before she could collect her thoughts, she heard that little voice inside her again. "Don't worry," it said. "Twenty thousand dollars for less than thirty seconds is the best thing you will have going in this lifetime. You have to milk this opportunity for everything you can."

"My God!" another voice said inside her. "What you are doing is simply prostitution! Not even Dianne would do this. Nothing good can come of this. Besides, it's is a violation of professional ethics. You could lose your license forever!"

At this point Carol realized she was having a true schizoid experience. Both voices were yelling inside her. Arguments pro and con were being shot back and forth. After a while she couldn't decide which voice made more sense. She silenced them both and prepared to leave.

CHAPTER 37
PAYBACK

Pretty soon her sessions with Maury became routine. She would start by talking to him about his seemingly endless problems with Kathleen and how to best deal with her. During the last five minutes of the session, she would then excuse herself for a moment and come out wearing a robe. He, in the meantime, would undress and cover himself with a towel. The entire routine never lasted more than a minute.

As he had promised, the money was sent to an offshore account in her name on the island of Berneau near the Grand Caymans in the Caribbean.

With Maury's help, she had set a corporation, Carol Lindsey, MA, Inc. She was the sole employee of the corporation. Maury was extremely knowledgeable about such arrangements and arranged everything for free. There were many benefits to such a setup. She did have to pay Social Security for both herself and the corporation. But she also was able to take a salary from the corporation and pay her taxes monthly. She set up a retirement account with herself as the sole proprietor of the money coming in. Also, with Maury's help, she—that is, her corporation—leased a new Mercedes.

Carol soon relocated her office on Park Avenue. Office rental was a legitimate corporate business expense, as was the furniture, office equipment, and a new secretary. Maury arranged for the secretary to come as an "independent con-tractor," thus saving Carol the hassle of withholding taxes and paying benefits.

All Carol's new outfits were tailored—both business and casual wear. No more of Dianne's hand-me-downs or pur-chases from the thrift shop. She began to shop at places she had only read about in the design section of the *New York Times*.

She reserved Fridays for her "therapy" sessions with Maury. Monday through Thursday was for her regular re-ferrals. This rapidly had begun to change, however.

Her new clientele was now largely drawn from attorney re-ferrals. Well-to-do people seemed to have as many prob-lems as her HMO patients. Why not simply capitalize on this? She was learning fast.

Carol had managed to retain the services of a well-known labor attorney who had taken a particular interest in HMO politics. He filed suit against the largest HMO in New York on her behalf, claiming fraud.

Facing several similar lawsuits, this HMO elected to settle out of court. With both real and punitive damages com-bined, her part of the settlement came to over $500,000. Carol mused over what could actually be accomplished with good legal help. *Just get a bigger shark*, she thought.

And she was right. Had this particular HMO been the least bit ethical, it would have saved a lot of money.

In the settlement, the HMO had agreed to continue referrals with the guarantee of timely reimbursement. Carol felt it would be a little hypocritical to accept such referrals. The money from her attorney referrals was a lot better. Just seeing a check from an attorney gave her an overwhelming sense of power.

CHAPTER 38
RUBEN GOLDBERG

R uben had initially been an employee of BBC when it was Blakemore & Cohen. He did not have the good looks or athletic build of some of his fellow colleagues; however, he was extremely efficient and very knowledgeable. He logged more hours than any of the other newer attorneys hired by Blakemore & Cohen. Despite this, he had been passed over for partnership on several occasions. After devoting seven years of his life to them, he left with nothing. He never forgot. Since that time, he built a very lucrative practice in the field of "family law" as was the euphemism for a divorce attorney. He loathed BBC. Upon learning the circumstances around Carol's divorce through court records, he could not resist calling her.

"Mrs. Berkowitz," he began, "my name is Ruben Goldberg. I represent women who have been given the short end of the straw from our legal system. I took the liberty of reviewing your case from court house records. I really feel this should be re-opened."

"I go by my maiden name, Ms. Lindsey," Carol began. "I

really have no desire to go through anything like I went through with John again."

"You won't have to," he persisted. "There are enough flaws in your settlement to make a first-year law student drool. The first thing," he went on, "is to revisit that DNA sampling."

"I've always known there was something wrong with that," Carol said. Ruben had now piqued her interest.

"Why don't you meet me for lunch this Friday? We could discuss it further."

They met at a fashionable Manhattan restaurant frequented by many of the more successful local attorneys.

"Mrs. Berk… I mean, Ms. Lindsey, I can tell you without reservation that the DNA is tainted. When I was an employee with Blakemore and Cohen, Mr. Bernado would cut my hair. The hair would land on the floor along with hundreds of other people's hair. From there it would get tracked around. Even though the shop was immaculate, any samples taken off the floor would have to be contaminated. I will agree to take your case for only a small contingency—no out-of-pocket expenses on your part."

On Carol's behalf, he filed for a request for case review, which was immediately granted. Upon realizing the hair sample was fraudulent, BBC tried to settle immediately, over John's objections. Evidential fabrication from such a prestigious law firm could have very serious consequences. Mr. Blakemore personally requested an immediate settlement to the limits of their liability.

Ruben extracted a seven-figure payment from BBC—

largely drawn from John's partnership funds. This was done with the understanding that the case would be sealed, never to be revisited. The partners of BBC did not wish to incur any future liability.

However, it was still not over for John.

Shortly after this settlement, BBC was served again by Ruben, now representing a young secretary by the name of Cindy Myers. Cindy was one of those very attractive blondes John could not keep away from. She was a paralegal with the firm. After he had been with her for a few months, he dumped her. With this she received her two weeks' notice with a lucrative separation package—a very common occurrence with John's "affairs."

Unbeknownst to John, Cindy had access to all the past records of BBC, including a list of the women John had "dated" and subsequently fired. Based on those records, she had picked up six other clients who were former employees of BBC.

Sexual harassment lawsuits were like dynamite. Even an inexperienced attorney in his or her first year of practice could ignite one. This time the settlement was in excess of 2.5 million. In addition, Cindy and her clients filed personally against John and managed to attach 15% of his future income.

John's status in the firm hit an all-time low, and he was quietly demoted to an employee. He was given a small office on the fifth floor. The B from BBC was removed from the front of the building.

In an attempt to maintain his lifestyle, he began to embezzle from his own firm. Having no level of sophistication in this, he was soon caught. This time, the charges were criminal. He waived a jury trial and, in turn, received a two-year sentence in a minimum security prison. His license to practice law was suspended for five years. All his accounts were frozen.

Since his divorce from Carol, he had gone from being one of the youngest partners in Blakemore and Cohen to becoming a guest of the state of New York. His income had dropped from the high six figures to zero.

When John did not present for evening roll call, guards were dispatched to find him. John Berkowitz, inmate #54891, was found lying unconscious next to the boiler in the laundry room. The guards attempted CPR, but to no avail.

The death was ruled accidental. "He must have fallen and hit his head," the guard volunteered. It was ruled an accidental death. The coroner agreed. No autopsy was performed. The bruises on his body were felt to be due to CPR, and the abrasions on his hands as well as his broken fingers went unnoticed. (Admittedly, a victim's fingers do not break during CPR.)

Carol got the call that night from Ruben. The news shocked her, but after reflecting briefly, she realized she felt nothing. She went into Jason's room. He was sleeping soundly. She kissed him lightly. "Maybe someday I will tell him. But not now..."

Shortly thereafter, the firm of Blakemore and Cohen collected on a $3,000,000 life insurance policy on John. Such life insurance policies are not unusual for full partners in a large firm. The policy was enforced as the premium had just been paid before John was demoted. No one ever thought to cancel it.

CHAPTER 39
THE ISLE OF BERNEAU

B erneau is an island about 30 miles west of the Grand
  Caymans. It is a small triangular speck on a map. But
it is a land of paradise to those who have lived and visited
there. The Hyatt Regency Enterprises leases one corner; the
Hilton leases the other. Both are rated as five star resorts.
The white sandy beaches and palm trees are very inviting.
Both the sunrises and sunsets are spectacular. The island has
a unique weather pattern that is as yet unexplained. The
temperatures are similar to the other tropical islands; however, the humidity rarely rises over 50%. Some climatolo-
gists attribute this to the "Coriolis effect"-a little-known
stream of air coming down a 50-mile corridor coursing north
to south as an atmospheric tide-somewhat similar to the jet
stream coursing east to west from Japan to North America.

The third corner of the island is the exclusive domain of
Jacques IV, the great grandson of the island's founder. The
mansion was built into a large cleft of solid rock. It has
been set afire by both the Portuguese and the French and
devastated by typhoons, but it has always come back more
sturdy and vibrant than ever.

As with most of the islands, Berneau has a very colorful and somewhat sordid past. It was originally settled by Jacques Berneau in the late 18th century. Jacques was a disinherited Frenchman, a senior bank officer specializing in loans to shipping firms dealing in overseas commerce. Unfortunately, an audit caught up with him, and he was exiled from France. What the audit did not catch was that he had set up several accounts in Spanish and Portuguese banks. The accounts were in the millions of francs, pesetas, and escudos. Most of his holdings were in gold.

Jacques purchased this remote island from the British government, who cared less about his history. After all, they were at war with France, and anyone paying them in gold was their friend. With the availability of slave labor, Jacques was able to build a thriving rubber plantation. Free trade was encouraged, and the island's economy flourished.

Jacques I, as he was later to be called, never married, although he impregnated roughly 60 of his female slaves. He would frequent the slave markets and pay huge sums for the most attractive female slaves. He did this for both his own pleasure and for the benefit of his male workers. He had learned a long time ago that the male species was much more obedient and productive if their basic needs were met. You could work them 18 hours a day if they knew the night would end with a pretty woman.

Jacques could not have been more correct. After less than ten years in the plantation business, he had become one of the richest men in all of the Caribbean.

The island had a small protected harbor from which all commerce emerged. At one time it was rumored that France tried to annex the island and tax Jacques' plantation. Three warships anchored just outside of the harbor to prevent any business from occurring until their demands of tax payments were met. To reinforce their point, they had fired several rounds onto the beach from their cannons, terrifying the residents. However, the French ships were heavy and could not come into the harbor itself without their hulls getting caught on the coral reefs.

Unbeknownst to the French, however, Jacques had anticipated just such a move from a foreign government. Some time earlier he had formed an alliance with a famous pirate, Jacob Marney, a former British admiral who had become disenchanted with England and had begun his own "trade" enterprise. He soon commanded four warships of his own and was doing quite well with the slave trade as well as plundering several French and Spanish galleons. He left the British alone. They, in turn, left him alone.

Under the cover of darkness and with the element of surprise, Captain Marney caught the French off guard and sank all three of their ships. It wasn't much of a contest. The French ships were difficult to maneuver and were unprepared for a confrontation. Marney's ships were lighter and more maneuverable. He was able to enter the harbor and attack the French from all sides.

Jacques paid him handsomely for his actions, but what he gave Marney was only a fraction of what he would have lost to the French government. France vowed revenge, but in the early 1800s they were having major problems with England, Spain, and Portugal. They had lost a lot of their "clout" and would have to be content with their current colonies in the Caribbean and in the Pacific Ocean.

After this, the island flourished autonomously and unchallenged. Soon, however, a very different problem arose.

At the age of 78, Jacques died abruptly—allegedly in the company of one of his favorite concubines. He was so enamored with his "special ladies," as he called them, that they had become a very privileged class. They were well educated by the foreign tutors that came and stayed on the island, and they enjoyed a very high standard of living. The women were basically treated like queens and princesses.

Jacques' death, however, created a major void in this thriving autocracy. There was a rush to control the finances and the island.

Mass confusion soon ensued, and the island's productivity dropped sharply. Family feuds, murder, and chaos took place over the next five years. It was only through the interdiction of Jacob Marney's oldest son, Clifford, that order was restored.

Clifford had originally been educated at Oxford, but chose to go to Boston to finish at the new business school on the Harvard campus. He had a keen mind and had done well with his father's business. He hit on a solution of simply issuing "shares" to all the island residents who could trace their lineage to Jacques. The rest were allowed to "buy in" over time, depending on their value to the island's businesses. In short, he began the first offshore corporation that was co-owned by both management and a privileged work force.

The exports resumed, and the island again flourished.

Clifford later married one of Jacques' daughters. Anna was a statuesque woman with blond hair and piercing blue eyes. They had one son, whom they named Jacques II.

Although Jacques II was a bit of a rogue, he married his favorite mistress just before the dawn of the 20th century. She gave birth to Jacques III. As was the case with Jacques II, he was educated on the island by European tutors. They would occasionally travel to Europe, the Far East, and the United States, mostly for business. However, the great majority of their time was spent on the island. On his last trip to the Far East, Jacques III fell in love with a Thai princess. They were married in a Buddhist ceremony on the island of Phuket.

On returning to Berneau, Jacques III devoted the rest of his life to building a mansion on the highest of the three corners of the island. This was to show his love for his princess. She bore him one son, Jacques IV.

Over the last century, Berneau profited heavily from both its rubber exports and its banking industry. Berneau was indisputably the richest island in the Caribbean. It was also the best kept secret.

Because of their genetic background, the true natives of the island have a distinctive, if not incongruous appearance. They have the strong, chiseled faces of the Europeans and the well-toned bodies of black athletes. Their names are a variation of French eponyms, and their language is a rich mixture of French and old English as well as native dialects. They number about 300. For the most part they are either bank or resort managers, having a significant amount of stock in each. In keeping with the Berneau tradition, they generally receive their advanced degrees in the United States. Lately, some had been studying in Europe.

The last few decades had seen a protracted construction boom—modern offices, mansions, resorts, and shops.

There were no less than ten thriving banks with strong ties to the United States, Europe, and South America.

The two five-star resorts on the remaining two corners of the island also generated a considerable income. These two resorts were not in any average listing and were generally booked over a year in advance, with rare last-minute openings for "special guests." The least expensive suite began at $5,500/day and went up from there. Considering all the amenities, it was felt to be very reasonable and, to this day, they are frequented by the rich and famous who want to be autonomous.

The banks are enterprises that are the sole domain of the natives. Anyone wishing to open an account would go through the most modern and exhaustive scrutiny. Any hint of fronting for organized crime or terrorism would be uncovered in such searches, and they would be summarily rejected. Ultimately, however, no private enterprise or government would ever be able to learn who held the accounts.

Depositors were paid a flat rate of 5%. The bank, in turn, was free to lend the money to legitimate businesses at much higher rates. The loan of one million dollars at 10% to a US corporation would yield them about $100,000 a year. You multiply this by the average of 2,000 loans per bank, and you have an idea of the net amount of money coming in to each of the ten banks on a yearly basis. This was only a small part of their income, however. The real income would come from speculative investments. This would be done jointly with a client and would frequently yield two to three times the original venture capital.

The government was autonomous and recognized by the United States and other major European countries, despite their frustration over the confidentially in their banking practices. Officials were elected by popular vote—all citizens, male and female, would vote.

Jacques IV was acknowledged as the supreme governor of the island. Nothing would ever transpire without his knowledge—at least up until now.

CHAPTER 40
JACQUES IV

J acques IV was a slim, handsome man in his early fifties. He had the tanned complexion common to most residents of the island of Berneau, but was a full shade lighter—a gift from his mother. He was well educated by the imported tutors. He was also a Kubota master—a form of martial arts unique to the island.

However, he had never married, and the government officials were starting to get worried. They did not want to see a repeat of the chaos in the early 19th century.

Carol knew nothing of the history of Berneau, let alone its unofficial governor. All she knew was that Maury had set up an offshore account. Every time she reviewed the monthly statement, the balance exceeded her expectations, even after all her expenses were paid.

The bank with whom she associated had asked if she would mind investing a small percentage of her account in "speculative" ventures. She agreed and every "endeavor" on their part yielded at least a 100% profit. Through Maury she had hired a financial consultant, a Mr. Benjamin Schwartz, who specialized in investments from offshore accounts.

She found her first meeting with Mr. Schwartz rather interesting. They met over lunch at one of the upscale restaurants in Manhattan. He was well groomed and appeared to be quite knowledgeable about money management. She could not help notice how he seemed to look at any attractive young lady who came within his view. She later learned he was a widower. He was always very business-like and gentlemanly. She did not really like the way he looked at her, however.

She once had a question of him and had called him personally. "It would be better if you met me for lunch for specific advice," he had said. "When you call me at the office I have to bill you two hundred dollars for every ten minutes of my expertise."

That's nothing, she thought. *I get one hundred times that for less than one minute of my "expertise."*

After the first year, she could have easily terminated the sessions with Maury, but she felt some sort of obligation to continue. It was amazing to her how life had changed so radically in the last 12 months.

During last Friday's "session" she noticed how much weight he had lost. On the rare occasion she opened her eyes, she no longer saw the rolls of flab.
She could actually see his abdominal muscles. "I've been going to the gym," he boasted. "I have also been sticking to a regular diet. This makes Kathleen mad, but I don't care."

The transformation was amazing. He was actually looking

athletic. Each week she began to see an improvement. His entire body had become muscular and toned.

He would no longer walk hunched over, looking at the ground. He would stand tall, his head held high. His short stature was hardly noticeable. Carol finally saw that he was actually taller than she. Most importantly, he smiled constantly. His entire demeanor had changed.

CHAPTER 41
CRISIS

Thursday afternoon Carol let her secretary leave early. As Carol was getting ready to leave, the phone rang. When she heard the voice on the other end of the phone, she froze.

"Ms. Lindsey," the voice began, "I just want to thank you for all you have done for Maury. He's so different. He doesn't complain, he smiles, and he is so affectionate to me that it is embarrassing. I finally just had to give in to him."

Carol breathed a deep sigh of relief. "That is nice to hear, Kathleen. Maury is a very good person."

"Well," Kathleen continued, "I thought maybe you could start seeing the both of us, and maybe we can work on our marriage."

Carol again froze. "I guess that would be possible," she began hesitantly.

"Since you always reserve Fridays for Maury, I'll come in

with him for a change. We'll see you then. I just don't know how to thank you. Whatever you have being doing has really helped. Good-bye."

Before Carol could utter a sound, the conversation was over. She fell back on to her couch. *I really hope you never learn what I have been "doing,"* she thought.

Friday morning arrived without fanfare. Carol arose as usual, helped Jason dress, and drove him to school.

"Good morning, Ms. Lindsey," his teacher said amiably. Mrs. Morris had replaced Ms. Starron as Jason's primary teacher. They now treated Carol quite like royalty. In addition to paying for the rest of the year, Carol had pledged a donation of $100,000 to the school itself. That was done with the understanding that Ms. Starron be transferred to one of the local satellite schools. Ms. Starron never knew what hit her.

Carol then went to her office to get ready for her session with Maury and Kathleen. She felt very uncomfortable. She had had her "session" with Maury just last Friday. It had gotten to be so routine she barely gave it any thought. She now knew this would come to an end.

She had no idea the matter had already been "handled."

At 8:55 a.m. the phone rang. Her secretary was frequently late, and Carol was used to answering morning calls.

"He's dead!" the desperate voice wailed.

"Kathleen?" Carol asked. "Who...?"

"They killed him!"

"Who?" Carol repeated. She could feel her throat go dry.

"Maury!" she wailed. "I found him in his study this morning. Could you please come over? There are a bunch of police and FBI agents here. I don't know what to do." She began sobbing.

"FBI?" Carol asked.

"Please," she begged, "just come over. I need help."

This was the first time this domineering woman had ever asked for help.

"I'll be right over." Carol's hands were shaking. FBI? She had no idea what to expect. But the feeling inside was not a good one.

Maury and Kathleen lived in a beautiful home in the suburbs just outside of the city. Carol arrived to see several police cars in the long driveway. Both uniformed officers and other "investigators" were milling about the house.

"Are you Carol Lindsey?" a plainclothesman asked sharply.

"Yes," Carol replied, trying to keep a professional demeanor.

"Please come with me," the man said.

He led her into what had been Maury's library and office. Out of the corner of her eye she noticed Kathleen in the living room, her head in her hands.

The library was in shambles. Several of the officers were sifting through the papers and books strewn about the office. There was blood on the far wall, with a larger pool on the floor. Cameras were flashing. In the corner she could see them zipping up a body bag.

"Please—sit," the man said.

"What ha…" she began.

"I'm Agent McCaffee, and this is my partner, Agent Rogers. We are part of the Justice Department investigating tax fraud."

"Tax…?" Carol's mind was in a tailspin.

"How long have you known the Lenowitzes?"

"Well over a year," she replied. "They came to me for marital counseling. That's my profession."

"From our records, only Mr. Lenowitz had been seeing you. You had regular Friday sessions with him."

"I started seeing them as a couple, initially," Carol began defensively. "It was only later that Kathleen dropped out. Maury wanted to continue with the sessions." She was visibly shaking.

"Can I get you anything?" the younger agent asked.

"No," Carol said, trying to compose herself. *How much do they know?*

"Do you see any other clients individually?" the senior agent went on.

"Sometimes…" she began carefully. She knew she was lying, and she knew they could tell. These people were no dummies and seemed to know a lot about her. "I felt he was suicidal," she continued. "I thought I could make a difference."

"Well," the agent said, "apparently you did. I understand Maury changed considerably while he was seeing you."

"Yes," Carol added with a faint smile. "I was going to start seeing them as a couple again. In fact, the appointment was for this morning."

She felt some relief that she could turn back to a more truthful track.

"What did you and Maury talk about during your sessions?"

The question sent chills down her spine. Did he really any know anything, or was he just probing? What if Maury kept a diary? The thought sent shudders down her spine. She was visibly pale.

"Are you okay?" the younger agent asked.

"No! Ninety percent of my net income just evaporated!" Carol felt like saying. Instead, she took a deep breath. "You say he was killed—in here?" She was attempting to gain some control of what seemed like an inquisition.

"Yes," the senior agent replied. "What did you and Maury discuss?"

"That would be privileged information," Carol began. "What we dis…"

"Ms. Lindsey," the senior agent said sternly, "the patient-client privilege applies only to attorneys and priests. This is a homicide investigation. You could be named as an accessory. Now, what did the two of you do during your therapy sessions?"

"We...that is... I did my best to boost his ego," she began, almost laughing inside.

"Be a little more specific," he said sternly.

"I just don't think it is proper to discuss it at this time. Maybe I should talk to a lawyer." She objected to the judgmental attitude of this man.

"You can get a lawyer if you wish," he shot back. "But he will just tell you to cooperate with us. We aren't interested in you specifically—at least not for the time being. If anything illegal transpired between you two, now would be the time to tell us. It would go much easier on you." Both agents towered over her. There was a harsh silence.

"Look, Ms. Lindsey," the more senior agent began more gently. "We have been on to Maury for some time. He was laundering money for several small-time city officials, getting kickbacks from construction contractors. Some of the larger payoffs involved federal government money. That's where we come in. We also have been investigating a connection between one of the contractors and another 'investor' who we suspect deals in narcotics. We estimate Maury was laundering between three to five million dollars a week.

"We think this is where the real money trail begins. As is usually the case, the government bureaucrats are just small game here. I'm sorry if we sound overbearing. We need to get to the bottom of everything that transpired. So far you are not a suspect. And, even if you were, we would not be directly concerned at this time. This whole thing is a lot deeper than you can imagine, and we are only interested in the big fish. Anything you could do to help us would be deeply appreciated."

"Well…I really don't know how to begin." Carol's throat was dry. She certainly was not about to tell them she had put over one million of this money into an offshore account, let alone what she did to get it.

"Maury came to me initially with Kathleen for counseling," she began carefully. "After a few sessions, Kathleen became impatient and ordered him to come see me alone, thinking he would be able to say or do things with me that he couldn't do with her around." She couldn't believe what she was saying, even though it was the truth.

"At first we really didn't accomplish much—that is often to be expected in these situations. However, once we went to a one-on-one schedule, I could see improvement." This also was true. She had just realized that she didn't have to tell them the details of how she would take off her clothes for what was literally a "one-on-one" session. It would only be logical to conclude that she was a good "therapist."

The remaining questions were handled easily. Carol began to feel quite relieved. When they told her she was free to go, she asked if she could see Kathleen.

"She has been placed in protective custody. Right now, I am not certain when you can see her," the agent said matter-of-factly. "There are some heavy hitters that have been losing a lot of money here. We are certain they will stop at nothing to get it back."

Protective custody? she thought to herself. She wondered if she had anything to worry about.

"We will be in touch," the younger agent said. "Feel free to call us. Here's my card."

CHAPTER 42
THE IRS

S oon, Carol got back into her regular routine. She would see clients Monday through Thursday. Friday was now her "free" day.

On one such Friday, Carol took Jason to school and went through the usual pleasantries with the instructors. She returned to the apartment Dianne had been subletting to her and began to thumb through the papers she kept on her offshore account.

Then came the knock at the door. The maids were there for the usual Friday housekeeping, and answered the door.

"Ms. Lindsey," one of them said in broken English, "the man at the door says you need to write your name so he can give you package."

Carol went to the door to see her postman. She had never met him before.

"Excuse me, ma'am," he began, "I need you to sign here...thank you."

The package was a brown envelope. She could see it was from the Internal Revenue Service.

"Dear Ms. Lindsey," it began, "we would like to arrange an appointment for a routine review of your listed corporate expenses. Please feel free to arrange for legal representation, should you so choose."

Her head began to pound.

Carol immediately called Mr. Schwartz. He agreed to have lunch with her that day. He had known Maury for the last five years and had thrived on his referrals. He told her he was devastated to hear the news.

Carol met him in the restaurant on the first floor of her office building. As they were sitting down, she thrust the IRS letter into his hands.

"What do I do?" She felt very panicky.

"Carol," he began reassuringly, "this is just an inquiry for income documentation. They simply want to know how you fund your corporate expenses—lease, auto expenses, employees costs, etcetera."

"But you know the checks come from my bank in Berneau," she replied. "No one ever has asked how the account was funded." Her head was pounding like a base drum.

"Well," he said thoughtfully, "we'll have to go to Berneau and see what we can present at the audit. Keep in mind, Carol, I have never lost a client to the IRS. Everything my clients have ever done is all perfectly legal." He smiled.

Like having sex every week at $20,000 a pop? Carol thought.

CHAPTER 43
THE FIRST VISIT

O n Monday, Carol and Jason flew directly to Berneau in a private Learjet. The runway on the island was considered too small for most commercial jets. Carol did not care how they got there. The weekend had been very unpleasant for her, not knowing what was in store.

Jason was thrilled with the idea of missing a few days of school to be with his mom. He loved the new computer games on the jet, and the three-hour flight went all too quickly for him.

Mr. Schwartz had reserved two suites at the Hilton. With such short notice, they were separated by two floors.

Carol had only read about the two resorts on the island. Seeing them totally took her breath away. They were huge architectural wonders built into the cliffs overlooking the water. Pools and waterfalls adorned the grounds. Each suite had a Jacuzzi fed directly from the water from the mineral springs. The sands on the beaches had an almost creamy appearance. The ocean was a clear blue green.

The drive to the bank was very short. The bank itself was modest by New York standards—not much floor space, three or four employees, several computers, and one manager.

Gerald Berneau was the manager of this particular branch. He was young, tanned, and almost too laid back. He greeted them at the door and escorted them to his office overlooking the inlet.

"You really don't need to document every cent that you transfer to us," he began. "We will fully cooperate with your government only with your permission. If we have to, we can generate papers for income documentation," he reassured her. "People come to Berneau to relax in our exclusive environment. Worries about taxes, fines, and the like must be left behind."

"I'll leave the work to Mr. Schwartz," Carol said. "That is why he is here. Jason and I would like to see the island, however."

"But of course," he said, smiling broadly. "And you cannot leave until you have met my uncle. He saw you come in today and would very much like to meet you. He is our unofficial governor and can solve many problems. All of you are invited to "The Palace" for dinner tonight."

The home of Jacques IV was frequently referred to as "The Palace." It occupied the third corner of the island and was every bit as luxurious as the two resorts.

At 6 p.m., Carol and Jason were escorted to the limousine Jacques had sent. She had been informed Mr. Schwartz would be occupied with business affairs, but might join them later. For an instant Carol thought she saw him on the beach with two of the island girls, but she was preoccupied with the thought of meeting the island's unofficial governor and paid it little notice.

Jacques met them on the veranda. Carol felt drawn to him, but immediately suppressed those feelings. She remembered what had happened in her past. *Still,* she thought, *maybe not all men are pigs. And even if they are, this is a choice tenderloin.* Her inner thoughts made her blush. Jacques noticed something, but did not say a word.

The evening was occupied with laughter, stories, and games. Jacques had one of his younger nephews, Jonathan Costanses, join them to round out the evening. Jonathan was about Jason's age. Jason told Jonathan about the computer games he played on the airplane, and the rest of the evening seemed to center to around that.

After a sumptuous dinner, they retired to the living room. The boys were delighted to see that Jacques had the same games on a computer hooked into his large screen.

"My dear," Jacques said, "you must take a walk on the beach with me. This is what I do every evening, and I hate to walk alone…"

They walked along what seemed to be an endless shoreline, the waves crashing only a few feet from them. The evening was warm, almost a little too humid for Carol. The breeze off the waves was enough to cool her, however.

Jacques had a talent for putting people at ease, and soon Carol was telling him everything about herself—almost everything, that is.

As they turned back, Carol tripped over a conch shell. Jacques quickly caught her. For an instant she was supported by his muscular arms. They were inches from each other, their lips almost touching.

Suddenly, she stiffened. "I'm sorry, Mr. Berneau," she said, trying to act aloof. "I very much enjoyed your hospitality, but I am not one of your island 'girls'—I'm not that easy." She could feel her forehead start to throb.

"My dear," he said, "please don't think so badly of me. I find you to be absolutely beautiful, but I would never take advantage of a woman as lovely as you, especially if I thought there was any chance you would be interested..." His voice trailed off.

They stood there, looking at each other, trying to feel each other's thoughts.

"Ah," he broke the silence, "we must be getting back. I am to be your personal tour guide tomorrow; everything has been arranged. I have a real surprise for you."

This was news to Carol. But it wasn't like she had made any plans. And Jacques seemed to be the perfect host.

CHAPTER 44
THE SURPRISE

J acques had arranged for Jason to spend the day at the home of Claudio and Andrea Costanses. The Costanses came from a highly respected lineage and could trace their relatives to the time of the founding of the island. The senior member of the family, Ramon, had been a bodyguard to Jacques III during the 1950s. He was killed protecting Jacques IV during a botched kidnapping attempt by four of the island henchmen. All but one were killed. The fourth somehow had managed to escape. They knew him only by his last name: Rinelli.

Jacques III had raised Ramon's only son, Claudio, as his own. When the time was right he had introduced Claudio to Andrea. It was love at first sight. They had five children ranging from five to 25 years old.

The first four hours of the day would be a mandatory session with one of the tutors. The rest of the day would be left for exploring, snorkeling, and, of course, computer games.

Jacques picked Carol up in one of his open-air limousines.

They were escorted down the steps as though they were royalty. They drove for a short distance to a home on one of the inlets—less than a mile from "The Palace." The two-story house was in a popular island design and overlooked the ocean. Carol could see a couple on the veranda. The woman stood up and waved as they came up the driveway.

Carol's heart stopped. "Dianne!" she yelled. They ran to greet each other—both began talking simultaneously, each keeping track of the other's conversation.

"After Ken and I got married here, we just could not leave. There was no reason to do so. Ken had opened his retirement account here thirty years ago—he told me we would never be able to spend it all. He still doesn't know me." She winked. "But he is a great husband and a fantastic companion. Jacques married us," she added.

The rest of the day was spent in nonstop conversation. They talked for hours. Carol had totally forgotten all her problems on the mainland.

"You should relocate your practice right here, Carol," Dianne said. "Rich couples need marital counseling as much as anyone. You could not find a better environment. New York is like a cesspool compared to this island."

Carol entertained the thought for a brief moment. The hectic existence of the city could be quite exhausting at times. Even in her new Mercedes, traffic was still traffic.

Carol also spent the next day with Ken and Dianne. This time Jacques had business in town. Carol suddenly realized she missed his company.

The following day, Carol, Jason, and Mr. Schwartz boarded

the Learjet for the trip home. Jacques greeted them just before they took off. He gently hugged her. Secretly she did
not want him to let go.

"My dear," he said with his soft voice, "I want you to have
this." He handed her what looked like a cell phone, complete with a charger. "It is a satellite phone. With this, you
can call me anytime of the day or night. I have programmed
in my number as well as the numbers of others you may
find useful." With that, he kissed her lightly on the cheek,
and bid her farewell.

CHAPTER 45
THE AUDIT

The next day, Carol drove Jason to his school and then made the short but hectic trip to her office.

Mr. Schwartz had left a message with her secretary—the IRS audit was scheduled for Friday morning. The agent had agreed to meet them at Mr. Schwartz's office. Carol began to feel a little queasy.

The agent was a pleasant man in his mid forties. He was thin and wore horn-rimmed glasses.

"Ms. Lindsey," he began. "You seem to have done quite well with your legal settlements. You paid your taxes appropriately. We have a comprehensive P&L statement from Mr. Schwartz on your income from your practice as well. What we cannot account for is the fact that your business expenses far exceed your gross income."

"I have provided some additional figures to explain that," Mr. Schwartz interjected, handing the agent a formidable binder. "Ms. Lindsey made some very prudent investments through a bank in Berneau. This generates a significant income. We have been trying to calculate the legitimate taxes on the income generated."

"I am familiar with the Island of Berneau," the agent said dryly. "How do you expect us to substantiate these figures?" he said, scanning the printouts he had been handed.

"Just look at this lovely young lady," Mr. Schwartz said amicably. "Does she look like one of your tax cheats?"

"Mr. Schwartz, tax cheats come in all sizes and shapes," the agent said sternly, secretly eyeing Carol's trim figure through her business suit. "I will be reviewing these figures with my supervisors. We will be in touch."

Mr. Schwartz smiled broadly. The session ended.

One month passed. On Friday morning there was a knock on the door. Again the maid came in. "Ms. Lindsey, someone at the door said you should make signature for package."

Carol opened the large brown envelope to see a 30-page printout. On the final page was a statement. "You have underpaid by $256,778. Please remit the sum in full within the next thirty days."

Carol was aghast. She immediately called Mr. Schwartz—a lunch meeting would be too far off.

"Don't worry, Carol," he said reassuringly. "I was expecting something like this. This is what you pay me for. Send me the papers and we will file for arbitration." A sickening thought flashed through Carol's mind. She remembered the last time she heard that word "arbitration."

One month passed. Carol again began to settle into her practice. The referrals were going quite well. The attorneys paid her promptly, and she felt she was able to help many couples with their problems. Several of the couples she worked with actually cancelled their divorce proceedings, much to the consternation of their attorneys.

Finally, she received another letter from the IRS. This time they had saved the cost of special delivery:

"Ms. Lindsey," it began. "After a full review of our documentation, we still feel you owe back taxes which, with penalty, come to $8,468.49. Please remit this in full within thirty days."

Carol felt as though a great burden had been lifted from her. She quickly wrote a check for $8,468.49 and put it in the mail.

CHAPTER 46
THE RINELLIS

Right after she got home with Jason, the phone rang.

"Ms. Lindsey," the gruff voice began, "you owe us some money. My father is Mr. Rinelli. We just wanted to say hello." The voice was chilling. "We are not the IRS. We do not 'arbitrate.' We will be in touch. Remember Maury…" The line went dead.

How could they know all this? she wondered.

Suddenly, the full scenario struck her between her eyes. Furiously she dug through her purse trying to find the card the FBI agent had given her. Instead, her hand ran over the cell phone from Jacques.

She waited until Jason had gone to sleep. Her hands were trembling. She looked at the menu—"Contacts." Jacques was speed dial #1. She punched it in. After three rings Jacques answered. "What is it, my dear?"

Suddenly, it was as though she had just left him. "Jacques," she stuttered, then began to cry.

Without going into the lurid details, she managed to get across to him that she had been the unwitting recipient of money from an organized crime syndicate, and now they wanted it back. The man calling had said his father was Mr. Rinelli.

"My dear," Jacques said reassuringly, "you have been away too long. We all miss you. I only met you two short months ago, and I have felt very empty in your absence. I will send my Learjet to pick you and Jason up tomorrow."

CHAPTER 47
BACK TO BERNEAU

Carol arranged for a limousine to take her and Jason to the airport the following morning. They drove straight out to where the Learjet was waiting. In less than three hours they were landing on Berneau.

Dianne and Ken met them at the airport along with Jonathan. She was told Jacques had some business to attend to but would be meeting them later.

Jacques had asked his trusted nephew, Gerald, to do some research on the Rinellis.

"They are not good people, uncle," Gerald began. "They are a very tight-knit family—two sons and the father. They are mostly into narcotics and city contracts. They tend to do all their own dirty work. They are disliked by the other families still doing business in New York, but they are also feared. Several years ago they tried to set up an account here."

146 · K. LYNCH

Jacques knew of the Rinellis quite well. Many years ago the senior Rinelli was among those who had tried to kidnap Jacques off the island and hold him for ransom. The senior Rinelli somehow eluded capture and fled to New York where he became rich in the narcotics trade. Only Jacques and the Costanses knew who had killed Ramon. His death would not be forgotten.

CHAPTER 48
SHOCK

Just before sunset, Jacques had all of them transported to his home on the point for dinner. It was sumptuous as usual. Ken and Dianne left early. "Now that we are old married people, we go to bed early—and sleep!"

Jacques and Carol walked alone on the beach, arm in arm. This time she did not hold back when he kissed her. She could not stop holding him. By the time they returned, both Jason and Jonathan were asleep on the couch. He gently picked up Jason and had the limousine take them back to the hotel.

Shortly after returning to her room, the phone rang. Thinking it was Jacques, Carol picked it up.

"No, you can't come up," she said, teasingly. "Jason is here."

Instead, she heard the same voice she had heard in New York.

"We just want to send you our greetings. We will be seeing you soon…"

Carol was beyond incredulous. *How did they know I was here?*

Without hesitation, she called Jacques. His maid answered. "Mr. Berneau is in the bath," she said flatly.

"Please," said Carol, "tell him to call me as soon as he can." Her head was pounding.

The next ten minutes seemed like ten hours.

"Yes, my dear." Carol heard his demure voice at the other end of the phone.
"I would have thought you would be asleep. Tomorrow, we have a lot planned for you and Jason…"

"Jacques!" Carol interrupted, her voice trembling, "Those people! They know I am here."

Jacques hesitated for a moment. "Don't worry, my dear." His voice seemed slightly more steeled. "I will look into the matter. Please, try to get some rest. I promise, no harm will come to you."

CHAPTER 49
CONNECTIONS

J acques pondered these circumstances well into the night. He had to tighten the island's security. To release another party's name and location was unheard of. Certainly he did not have direct control over the people hired by the two resorts; however, there was a leak that had to be fixed.

Jacques made several calls that night, including those to his contacts in the Grand Caymans. Most flights to Berneau came from the Caymans. It was rare that a direct flight from the states would be cleared. He left strict orders at the small airport on Berneau—all flights in and out would undergo maximum scrutiny.

Mr. Rinelli and his sons landed in the terminal on the main island in the Grand Caymans the following morning. From there they chartered a flight to Berneau for early afternoon.

Their pilot was James Costanses, the oldest son of Claudio and Andrea. By the age of 25, he knew the islands of the Caribbean like the back of his hand. Except for a four-year stint in the army as an airborne ranger, he had lived there all his life. He knew of the circumstances of his grandfather's death. His arduous training at Ft. Benning was about to be put to good use.

James met the Rinellis in the bar at the small airport. He could see they had been drinking heavily. He followed them as they staggered toward his aircraft, smelling of cheap Chianti.

"Do you think you can get us to the island in one piece in this thing?" the older Rinelli blurted out rudely. James did not respond.

The aircraft was an older twin engine Wellcraft. Since the 9/11 tragedy, it had been altered such that the pilot could enter the cockpit independently from the passengers. The pilot's cabin was separated from the passengers' by a locked metal door.

The aircraft departed at exactly 4 p.m. No one saw it take off. No flight plan was filed. This was not particularly unusual in the laid-back atmosphere of the Caymans.

As he reached his altitude of 10,000 feet, James turned toward the specified coordinates and flipped on the autopilot. He checked his passengers through a small closed circuit screen. They were all sprawled in their seats in a drunken stupor. He then donned the only parachute in the aircraft and exited the cockpit. James allowed himself to freefall for the first 8,000 feet before opening his parachute. His passengers continued to sleep, undisturbed, totally unaware of his exit.

Claudio Costanses took his boat from the island that afternoon. He entered the predetermined coordinates into the boat's GPS. The rendezvous would be 30 miles off the coast. He looked up as James skillfully manipulated his ram-air parachute to land 20 feet from the boat. He was in the water for less than one minute.

The Wellcraft was last seen by the Costanses as a small speck heading toward the horizon. *The debt has been paid,* they thought silently. *May Ramon now rest in peace.*

CHAPTER 50
SEDUCTION

Carol slept fitfully the night before. At any moment she expected the man with that awful voice to burst through the door.

Jacques met her at the hotel that afternoon. "My dear," he began, "you should not allow yourself to get so upset. I give you my personal word of honor—you will never hear that voice again."

Carol was unaware that the matter had been handled.

"I want you to try our special island drink." He smiled. "It is my own personal recipe. It is a secret mixture of light and dark rum blended with our passion fruit extract we make on the island."

"Jacques, I can't return to New York. At least not in the near future," she said, her voice still shaking. "Jason and I will never be safe."

"You will be safe here," Jacques replied firmly. "I think

you should give serious consideration to Dianne's suggestion and relocate your practice. Your clientele could stay at one of our resorts. I might even be able to arrange a 'package.'"

"What about my license?"

"My dear," he laughed. "I am the president of Consumer Affairs for the island. I am the only one who can grant licensure to legally practice on the island."

Carol could feel herself relaxing. The drink was having its desired effect. Finally, curiosity got the best of her. "Is there anything you cannot do?" she inquired.

"I really don't think so, my dear," was his reply. His broad smile enhanced his chiseled features.

They had a sunset dinner on the hotel's veranda. After a third glass of the island blend, Carol was totally "relaxed." Jason had again asked to spend the night at the home of Andrea and Claudio, where he and Jonathan played their computer games well into the night.

At sunset Jacques and Carol walked along the tide pools on the shore of the resort. She could not take her eyes off his handsome, rugged face. She could not help wonder about his past—and his history with women. She knew it was not right to ask. I mean, what if he were to ask her about her past?

"I have only known this man for less than two months," she resolved. "Whatever he did before then is not important to me. Tonight he is mine."

They walked for some time by the tide pools. She could

hear the waves thunder in the background only to be interrupted by the staccato calls of the seagulls.

With the setting of the sun he escorted her to her suite. The windows had been opened to let in the evening breeze.

He kissed her lightly and turned to leave. This time Carol did not let go. Her arms encircled his taut waistline, and she began to kiss him passionately. Jacques, the consummate ladies' man, was now the prey. And Carol was not going to let him escape. Years of physical and emotional suppression began to unravel. She pushed him onto the bed and pulled him close to her, rendering him helpless. Her linen dress slipped off easily.

In a brief moment she removed all his clothes. They lay together, locked in a passionate embrace. She then rolled on top of him, pinning him to the mattress. Her body quivered in pure ecstasy as she took him in and thrust herself against him with total abandonment. She could feel her entire body shaking. Between gasps she could hear herself moaning uncontrollably. They merged as one. She did not stop until she felt him become totally limp and he lay there like a fallen leaf. She snuggled against his furry chest, savoring all of his warm, sensuous body. She felt more content than she ever had been.

Yes, there would be a tomorrow. The sun would come up. Her practice here on Berneau would flourish. The FBI files on the Rinellis would simply sit and gather dust. She and Jason would be safe. She might even return to New York on occasion—but only to visit.

But for now, she was with the man of her dreams...

The tropical breezes gently moved the sheer curtains back

and forth as if to blend with her inner feeling of contentment.

Day blends into night. Time now stands still.

The End

Printed in the United States
115359LV00003B/232-234/P

9 781432 726508